FLIRTING WITH DANGER

"Now the next thing to learn is how to flirt with your partner."

"I don't flirt," I said firmly.

"Well, I agreed to help you, didn't I," Lucas returned cheerfully. "You'll learn."

"But I don't want to fl—"

"Ah, Miss Canning, your eyes are stars, your lips—"

"Lucas, please don't—!" I pleaded, my heart hammering, for his voice sounded too sincere for comfort. To my indignation, I saw he was laughing at me. "Why you—"

"But stay, my heart! Does Miss Canning care if I am sincere or not? Each word that falls from her lips is a die that determines the fortunes of my heart—" he declaimed theatrically.

"Oh, stop it, " I said. "You know that any future connection between us is all in Mama's head, so I wasn't piqued at all. I was—was merely relieved that you *were* play-acting."

He still smiled, but an intent look grew in his eyes as he gazed at me.

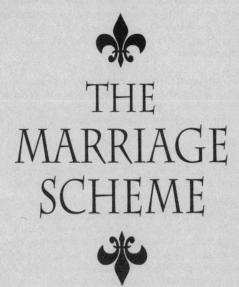

THE
MARRIAGE
SCHEME

KATHLEEN ELLIOTT

HarperPaperbacks
A Division of HarperCollins*Publishers*

HarperPaperbacks   *A Division of* HarperCollins*Publishers*
                    10 East 53rd Street, New York, N.Y. 10022

Copyright © 1994 by Karen Eriksen Harbaugh
All rights reserved. No part of this book may be used or reproduced in any manner whatsoever without written permission of the publisher, except in the case of brief quotations embodied in critical articles and reviews. For information address HarperCollins*Publishers*,
10 East 53rd Street, New York, N.Y. 10022.

Cover illustration by Bob Berran

First printing: August 1994

Printed in the United States of America

HarperPaperbacks, HarperMonogram, and colophon are trademarks of HarperCollins*Publishers*

❖ 10 9 8 7 6 5 4 3 2 1

I'd like to dedicate this book to my family: my parents for their belief in me; my mother- and father-in-law for laughing at all the funny parts in the story; and my husband, John, and my son, Derek, for believing that I could really write a book and not complaining about my long sessions with my book. Last but not least, I'd like to thank my critique group (Mary, Pamela, and Teresa) for their encouragement and for catching all the teeny (and not so teeny) little errors I missed in the heat of composition.

1

It was not that I disliked being at Miss Ang-stead's Seminary for Young Ladies, despite the other girls' snobbishness, though that was what some might have thought. I even enjoyed my room, for I was a parlour boarder and had it all to myself, with my name, "Georgia Canning," painted on the outside of my door. It was austere; its one concession to decoration was a half-length mirror on the inside of the door. I did not look at it much, for I knew what I would see: chestnut-brown hair, pale skin, and a light (*very* light, thank goodness!) sprinkle of freckles over my nose. My face was not classically oval like my mother's, for I had a small pointed chin, and my eyes were as green as a cat's. Mama often said my face was heart-shaped, but I think she was only being kind.

As for my clothes . . . well, they were nothing to look at, either, for all of us wore the schoolgirl's uniform of white, cream, or grey round gowns that covered us from neck to toe. Mine fit me only for the few months I grew into them. Then I would be given another larger one that would bag around my figure until I grew into *it*. I never paid much attention to fashion anyway, so I ignored my appearance unless it was untidy.

It was just that, as I grew older, I became more and more aware of Mama's single state and how unusual it was. Other girls' mothers were not as pretty as mine, but they were married. I watched Mama when I was home and kept note of her letters. The faces in Mama's salons changed, but I noticed a persistent one—a man she called Sir Jeremy. Mama's letters usually mentioned him once or twice. Finally, when I had just turned seventeen, a letter came that mentioned his name ten times. Nothing remarkable in the letter about him—merely that they had gone to the opera and then to someone's ball, and some of his thoughts on Reform.

From my window at school, I saw the older girls depart Miss Angstead's Seminary for Young Ladies to have their Season in London or giggle to each other when passing a handsome Hussar in the street. My thoughts turned—not unnaturally—to marriage, and the heretofore unthinkable idea came to me: Could it be possible that even at the advanced age of six-and-thirty, my mother might marry again?

This shocked me a little, for six-and-thirty was

a great age: surely past the time of falling in love. It was difficult to think of my mother giggling behind her hand and flirting with her eyes in the way some of my schoolmates did when they had a *tendre* for some young man. Yet I heard of some of those same schoolmates' widowed mothers remarrying, too, and they not much older than my own mother. I was determined to quiz Mama on this the next I saw her.

As Mama was preparing to leave my room at Miss Angstead's after a visit, and after she mentioned four or five appointments with Sir Jeremy for the next month, I said bluntly: "Mama, are you going to marry Sir Jeremy Swift?"

She looked at me, startled, and blushed. "Good Lord, Georgia, how you take one up!" She fussed with her reticule and rose from the chair next to my bed.

I put my hand on her arm, and she sat down again. "Mama, I am seventeen now, no longer a little girl. You have increasingly mentioned Sir Jeremy in your letters, and now you have five appointments with him this month. If he might become my father, perhaps I should know."

"I—I haven't accepted him," she said in a low tone. She turned her face away. "He comes from an old and well-known family. What could I bring to him, do for him? I merely have enough to support you and me, and my family was neither illustrious, old, nor rich. He *should* marry a respectable young woman who would do him credit—as I cannot."

"How *can* you say that, Mama! I should think

that anyone would be proud to have you to wife!"

She smiled at me with affection, but the wistful-ness did not leave her eyes. "Thank you, my love. But you see, my father was a merchant—and not a rich one at that. I could not bear to have Sir Jeremy estranged from his family; your father and I loved each other dearly, but I know how much it hurt him to be cut off from his family. I do not want to have that happen again. You can understand that, can you not?"

I did and said so. I also thought Mama had too many scruples. If Sir Jeremy had no qualms about proposing to her—and I supposed he was old enough to know his own mind—I did *not* see why she should have any about accepting. But I did not think Mama would see it this way, so I said nothing.

"Besides," she continued with a bitter laugh, "how am I to know he isn't merely trifling with me?" She pressed a hand to her temple. "It is *so* complicated. I have been disappointed before. It is hard for me to trust anymore, I think. What if he was merely dangling the idea of marriage in front of me so that I would be less inclined to look else-where?" She closed her lips firmly, glancing at me, then let out a sigh. "Ah, my dear, I love him, but I couldn't bear to think he would turn out like so many others."

"Exactly." I put my arms around her shoulders. "I feel it is my duty—since your father has died and Grandfather Canning has cast us off—as nearest kin, to see if this man is really fit to become your husband and my stepfather. After all," I said, affecting a haughty pose, "we deserve nothing but the best."

The trick worked: Mama laughed. "You are a funny one!" But her eyes were still sad. "You have been lonely, have you not? I have not done well by you, I think. I am a foolish woman, my dear."

All my maternal instincts were born in that instant. Poor Mama—so wise and at the same time so foolish! "I don't really care to make friends with the silly girls here at school—they can be tedious at times. I enjoy reading much more. And if I come home more often, both of us will be less lonely." A scheme was growing in my mind in which I would be doing more than coming home, but I'd think of that later. "Tell me more of Sir Jeremy."

"Oh, my love!" Mama hugged me in a rush of silk and perfume. "Well, if you insist—I believe you have met him once or twice."

I nodded. To my surprise, I remembered him as one whom I liked more than the others. He took notice of me where the others did not, and he had been very polite. I hardened my heart against him, however; I would see what his intentions were regarding my mother first before being fooled by any charm he cared to exude.

I smiled. "Yes, I remember him. I hope I may see him again sometime."

"Ah, you will. I shall make sure I invite him to dinner the next time you are home." The clock on the wall chimed, and Mama jumped and looked at it. "Oh, dear, I must go or I shall not get back to London before Monday. . . ." Tears came to her eyes again, and she searched for her handkerchief. She had left it on the chair, and I brought it to her. "You are too good to me, my dear. I do not know what I have done to deserve such an understanding daughter. Well. I must go." I was hugged again, and after I gave her a kiss, she left in a rustle of skirts.

In the end I had to simulate as many symptoms of an interesting decline as possible so I could go home immediately. Goodness knows I wouldn't have been allowed to go home if I *asked*—it simply wasn't done. And so I set myself to planning how I would leave Miss Angstead's Seminary for Young Ladies.

I would be cautious, I told myself. Too many girls had been caught play-acting an illness immediately after vacations and holidays. I did not want to risk anyone thinking I was play-acting, too.

Whenever the weather looked threatening, I took the opportunity to stroll the gardens around the school, saying—if anyone warned me that a storm was building—that the gardener told me his bones said otherwise. A lie, of course. Old Jake was always accurate about changing weather, but I quelled any feelings of guilt by reminding myself that this deception was for Mama and my future. A wetting did not work, however; I became soaked to the skin, received a scold from whatever schoolmistress caught me, and was forced to take a hot bath. I emerged from this with a heightened color—of health, not fever.

I progressed from lying to theft. I stole apples from a nearby orchard to eat first thing in the morning. Eating fruit for breakfast, guaranteed Miss Angstead's cook, would cause the flux and promote influenza. I faithfully ate apples for a month and a half, but all I did was lose some baby fat and feel healthier than I had before. Looking in the mirror at my thick and glowing hair, shining green eyes, and daisy-fresh skin was almost enough to cast me into despair.

This would have been discouraging to a girl of lesser mould, but I was persistent and had the strength of conviction that in the end this would be for the good of all concerned. It came about— indirectly, however—that I owed my eventual appearance of decline to Emily Possett.

Emily was a likable girl who was not so high in the instep as to avoid my company. She was also an inveterate gossip: since she kept company with the "select" group of girls, I would hear of those in the highest circles of the ton. Emily, not having anyone else with whom to discuss these things, often came to me.

I was sitting cross-legged on the bed, reading Plutarch's *Lives,* and was getting heartily bored of it. I had discovered a separate store of books at Miss Angstead's when I first became a parlour boarder. It was a large, closetlike room, just down the hall from mine. It was never locked, and curious, I took it upon myself to peek within: primers on Latin, Cicero, Plato, Rousseau, Wollstonecraft. I convinced myself that no one would notice one or two books missing, if I shuffled some others loosely together to cover the empty spaces.

Emily knocked at my door and came in. Sometimes I found the goings-on of the upper 500 somewhat tiresome, but this time it was a welcome change from the *Lives*.

"Oh, Georgia, the most appalling thing!" exclaimed Emily, flinging herself at the bedpost and clutching it with all the fervor of a saint clinging to the cross. She rolled her eyes toward heaven, and I was reminded of a picture I once saw of the ecstasy of St. Agnes. I often thought that if the stage had been a respectable occupation for a lady, Emily would have been a female Kean. Her dramatic good looks and talent for histrionics were going to be wasted on a future society matron.

"Only think!" she breathed. "Lord Hawksley has *poisoned* his wife!"

I patted the bed beside me, and she somehow managed to fall upon it in a remarkably decorous manner. She supported her chin in her hand and gazed at me expectantly.

I lifted a skeptical eyebrow. "No doubt she ate something that disagreed with her," I said.

Emily seemed somewhat daunted by this but persisted. "Oh, no! It was a definite case of poisoning. Lady Caroline told me so. She said that he only married Lady Hawksley for her money, and had fallen in love with another—some say it is Sophia Penningsley—and thus she was an Impediment to his Desires! Lady Hawksley, I mean."

"And so poor Lady Hawksley exits this life unmourned," I said flippantly.

Emily gave me a reproachful look. "Well, I don't know. Caroline says she also was in love with someone else, so I suppose *he* must mourn her.

Not that anyone *should* mourn her, because she isn't dead." She considered this for a moment. "Not yet, anyway."

"I thought you said she was poisoned."

"She was! Only, she suspected it and called the servants. She is only in a decline now. I suppose they must have given her ipecac to get the poison out," she said knowledgeably.

"Ipecac?"

"It's horrid stuff. My youngest brother had to take it once when we found he had the bloody flux. It made him vilely ill and he simply *retched* all over the place."

"Really, Emily!" I said, nauseated. I had an odd feeling that something was important here, but I was too distracted to hunt down this idea.

"But it got all the poison of the flux out of him. That is why it works. It makes one give up one's dinner, and the poison, too. Most households have it to take care of the disease, but one can use it for plant poisons, too."

I shuddered. "No doubt." I turned the subject, hoping Emily would take the hint. Having got a satisfactory reaction from me, she complied.

She chatted amiably on, and I floated off to other thoughts. She mentioned Sir Jeremy Swift once, and my mind came to attention, but it was merely in reference to his wealth. Apparently he, along with Lord Hawksley, moved in the highest circles. My mind kept insisting there was something important about Lady Hawksley, and groping toward that thought, I came to it—ipecac!

I turned the subject again, enquiring about

Emily's family. She talked cheerfully of her brother's toothache and her mother's Interesting Condition. I reflected aloud that it was fortunate her father was a physician and knowledgeable about these things. She agreed.

"I suppose that is how you came to know about the ipecac," I said casually.

"Yes! Father is always telling me about remedies he uses. He thinks ipecac should always be available in case of need."

I wondered privately how often people were poisoned by their spouses to warrant such a recommendation but concluded it must be more for the flux than ridding one's self of a husband or wife.

"Indeed, when last Father visited me, he brought a bottle of it for the infirmary here," said Emily.

"I imagine since it is used in urgent circumstances, it must be in the unlocked cupboard there."

"Well, of course!" she exclaimed. "Miss Lauderdale would hardly want to fumble with a lock when someone is at Death's Door!" Miss Lauderdale was the natural science mistress, which meant she pointed out flowers and plants and had us sketch them. She was also in charge of the infirmary.

It was half an hour before dinner then, and we parted to ready ourselves for it. Not that I *felt* ready when I sat down to dinner. I pushed the jellied eel about on my plate and glanced at Emily. She ate with her usual hearty appetite. I grimaced. There must be something about physicians' daughters that accustoms them to vivid descriptions of the effects of ipecac.

*   *   *

Because my next operation was more perilous than any of my other attempts at becoming ill, list making was imperative. First, because I did not want to take the whole bottle, I needed a container for the ipecac. I thought my tooth cup would suffice for now. Second (and I congratulated myself for my detailed planning), I would oil the hinges on the infirmary cupboard in case it squeaked. After mentally searching my belongings, I remembered I had a bottle of camellia oil for the hair. It smelled pleasant, so I did not think anyone would detect it.

Third, caution. Miss Lauderdale had a connecting door to the infirmary. I did not know if she was a heavy sleeper, so I had to assume she was a light one. The infirmary, I knew, was usually unlocked. I would have to take my chances on that. Most important, I had to have a reason for being out of my room at night. I thought of several (a burglar, nightmares, and the like) and discarded them all. The simplest was the easiest: that I felt ill.

When Miss Standish checked to see if I was asleep, I must have seemed dead to the world. I waited two hours. Then, as quiet as a cat, I crept out of my room.

I met with no hindrance. The infirmary door was conveniently unlocked, but so was the connecting door. I hesitated. Perhaps my candlelight might wake Miss Lauderdale! I would have to risk it: this was for Mama.

When I stood by the cupboard, I heard Miss Lauderdale moan in her sleep on the other side of the door. I froze. But silence for the next long moment reassured me, and putting my candle on the floor, I began oiling the hinges.

The cupboard door opened without a squeak. By the light of the candle on the floor, I could make out the simple block letters naming the object of my search. Casting another look toward the connecting door, I quickly opened the bottle of ipecac and shook a fifth of its contents into my tooth cup. Carefully, I replaced the bottle and closed the cupboard.

Clutching the cup, I crept out of the infirmary and ran as quietly and quickly as I could without spilling the ipecac. When I had gained my room, I shut the door and leaned against it, feeling as if I had held my breath during the entire operation. My heart was beating rapidly; I took a deep breath to calm it. I let it out with a *whoosh* and allowed my shaking legs to take me to my bed.

I stared at my booty for a while. My campaign would begin tomorrow, but I was curious. I sniffed the powder. No real scent to it; was it tasteless as well? I wet my finger with a bit of it and put it to my tongue. Gahh! Immediately I went to the pitcher by my bed and drank some water to wash out the bitterness. It was going to be difficult to down the stuff, but I felt equal to it. There is nothing more determined than a Canning bent on action, Mama always said of Father, and I knew this was true for me, too.

I set my tooth cup under my bed. The maid never swept under there anyway, so it would be safe. As I got into bed, I reflected that I had an old perfume vial into which I could pour the stuff. But then I yawned hugely and consigned this task to the morning.

I awoke with a feeling that all was not right. I had not much time to ponder over this, for suddenly all sleepiness left: my stomach turned over. My mind immediately went to the ipecac. Is this all it took to make one ill? I did not want to be sick now! I waited anxiously for more violent signs, but nothing else appeared; I remained nauseated until exhaustion overtook me, and I slept.

I staged the first display of my illness for Sunday. In most girls this would have been suspicious, but I was fond of going to church, and this fact was well known. I did not have a reputation for piety, however; it was also well known that I went because I loved the music springing from the pipe organ like winds from the sea. The schoolmistresses knew only the most extreme circumstance could tear me from this treat. So it was with concern that the Headmistress, Miss Angstead, listened to me when I complained of feeling a little faint.

She pushed back her unruly grey-white hair and looked at me with her sharp but kindly brown eyes. My lack of sleep supported me: shadows darkened my eyes, and I looked pale. I blushed a little at the lie, and she laid a bony hand on my forehead, apparently thinking I had the flush of fever.

She gazed at me thoughtfully. "You do not feel warm," she said. "Perhaps the walk to the church will revive you." She patted my cheek. "You have a good constitution; I am sure you will feel better shortly."

I felt ashamed at deceiving her, but neither this nor her insistence that I attend church kept me from my plan. I had secreted a stoppered vial, which contained the ipecac and water, in a pocket of my dress. My experience the night before warned me of its potency, and I did not want to be as violently ill as Emily's brother. I hoped I had diluted it enough to make me an interesting color, but not enough to send me to bed.

The sermon as usual was dull, but I kept awake for the music. I decided to sip the vial during the last hymn; that way, some people would be busy singing and the rest would be busy watching our new curate-from-London's way of conducting the choir. Last week he crouched down when the choir was to sing *piano* measures and suddenly leaped like a tiger upon its prey (the choir) at *forte,* arms outstretched. Today he looked as if he were pantomiming a windmill. I waited.

The curate's thin arm sprung in an electrified manner into the air and suspended there. This was my cue. As his twitching fingers took riveting command of every eye, I coughed, and under my handkerchief I quickly sipped the vial. I glanced around surreptitiously and caught Schoolmistress Lauderdale's glare. My hand shook as I stoppered the vial under my handkerchief, wondering if she had seen me drink from it. She only looked at me for a moment, however, before turning, a besotted mist settling over her face as she gazed at the curate. I felt relieved; the rumor must be true that Miss Lauderdale had a *tendre* for him. No doubt my cough had distracted her from her reverie. I sneaked a glance at the younger Miss Standish and noted that she, too, looked dreamy. So that was true, too! I saved the information for later: I would have something to tell Emily for a change.

The potion took longer to work than I thought; I had planned to look ill while all of us from Miss Angstead's walked down the church steps. We had already made our curtsies to the vicar when I felt my stomach turn. I prepared myself to look interestingly pale.

I was not prepared to become violently sick. I only had time to moan to Miss Standish in front of me before I retched all over the hem of her dress. I heard a revulsed shriek as I doubled over and gave up jellied eel again. A thought flashed through my mind that if I had to heave, I was glad it was on Miss Standish instead of Miss Lauderdale. I liked Miss Lauderdale. Miss Standish was snobbish.

The next hour flashed by quickly. I saw the worried faces of Miss Angstead, Miss Lauderdale, and the curate hover over me. I felt myself being carried and deposited in someone's carriage, but any gratitude I fostered at being able to lie down was quickly quashed as we bumped down the road to Miss Angstead's.

I could do nothing but moan, cough, and choke as I was undressed and put to bed. I tossed and turned therein, acting for all the world as if I were in a high fever. I felt sure Death was going to catch up with me, and I wished he would hurry up about it. It was not until my stomach was done mauling the rest of me that I lay still, sipped something that someone put to my lips, and fell asleep, aching.

I still felt ill in the morning, but better the next day under Miss Lauderdale's ministrations. I protested weakly that I did not need so much fussing, and Miss Angstead retorted that I should be grateful that Miss Lauderdale was helping. Miss Lauderdale actually smiled broadly at this, which surprised me, for she was a solemn young woman and her shy smiles were sweet but rare. I admired her when I first came to Miss Angstead's and used to imagine tragic and romantic stories about her to justify her single state. So I felt embarrassed that she should use her valuable time taking care of me in my induced illness.

I mumbled my thanks to her, feeling ashamed, but she smiled and shook her head. "You may not know it, but I owe you something as well. It was the least I could do to repay you." I wondered at this, but not for long, as I yawned and fell into sleep again.

As the days passed, I grew stronger but was still interestingly pale and wan. I tried to sustain this as long as I could (without ipecac), but my pink cheeks soon betrayed me. When Miss Lauderdale reported to the Headmistress that I was well enough, I was called to her room.

I twisted my hands in front of me nervously, not knowing what this interview was about. Miss Lauderdale had been evasive when I asked her. Miss Angstead was writing something as I sat and did not look up at me until she finished with a flourish.

She sat back in her chair then, steepled her fingers, and looked at me for a long moment. Her dark, sharp eyes assessed me, and she seemed to come to a decision. She pulled open a drawer and tossed something onto her desk. It was the vial I had carried with me to church. I flushed hotly.

"You know what this is," Miss Angstead said softly. It was a statement.

I looked down at my hands. "A vial?" I murmured vaguely, trying to sound as though I were only guessing.

Miss Angstead emitted what sounded very close to a snort. "Come, come, my dear. You are intelligent enough to translate Plutarch, you do not need to guess what this object is. I imagine this has something to do with your late illness?"

I suffered a severe shock. Not only had she discovered the vial, but it seemed she knew all along of my depredations in the small closet-library. I took myself well in hand, however. I opened my eyes wide with innocence and looked at her appealingly. She considered me with her intelligent eyes, gave back an amused smile, tapped her steepled fingers together, and waited for my answer. She had an efficient air that gave the impression of having all the time in the world. I knew then I was up against a seasoned campaigner. I wanted to cry in despair at the mess of my plans but resolutely took hold of my bottom lip with my teeth and managed not to. I would think of other plans.

"It held ipecac, ma'am," I said, looking at her defiantly.

"Ipecac. I do not see how that substance could have been useful in Church."

"Well, it wasn't, not in Church. I only meant to take enough to be thought in a decline."

"A decline. And why was it necessary to go into a decline? Not to avoid your studies, I hope?"

"Oh, no, Miss Angstead! Ask anyone! I really do like my studies. It was for my mother."

"Your mother." Her habit of echoing me made me nervous. I shifted from one foot to another. She indicated that I should choose a chair. I sat gingerly on the edge of one. "Would not a decline make your mother anxious more than anything else?"

"Well, yes, it would for a while until I became better. You see, I need to go home. She needs me to take care of her."

"Mrs. Canning, I suspect, is quite old enough to take care of herself, do you not think?

"No! I mean, no, ma'am. She's quite alone, without proper company, and it's horribly easy for unscrupulous people to take advantage of her. It has happened before, you see," I said fiercely. "She doesn't have anyone except me, really."

"From what I hear, your mother doesn't lack for company." It was said kindly, without malice, but I felt despondent.

"But not *proper* company!" I blurted. I blushed again.

"And you think by leaving school, you will be repaying her," she said conversationally.

"No, that is not it at all." I decided the only way out of this was to explain how I had come to decide on my plan. I related to her Sir Jeremy's proposal to my mother and her refusal.

Miss Angstead listened and made no comment.

I felt comforted by this, somehow. I finished my tale, and she sat there nodding, seeming to think. "And how did you—procure—the ipecac?" she asked. Hanging my head, I told her my preparations and actions. She raised her eyebrows, but she seemed amused rather than angry. She said dryly: "Miss Lauderdale told me not to underestimate you."

"Miss Lauderdale?"

"Yes. She was the one who found your vial. No, she did not intentionally betray you," she assured me as I shot her an indignant look. "She thought you had taken the potion inadvertently, or worse, and she was in fear for your life."

"I wouldn't—"

"No, I know that now, but I also know how mean-spirited some of the other girls can be, and why your mother wanted you to be a parlour boarder. It is often reason enough for girls to be despondent. And, after all, taking the potion was a rather desperate act, don't you think?"

I twisted my fingers, and muttered agreement. I looked up again at her pleadingly. "But, don't you see, desperate situations require desperate acts to solve them! I know I can do something to make Mama's situation better! I have to go home!" My voice cracked.

Miss Angstead sighed. "And what do you suppose you will do, once you are home?"

I looked at her steadily. "Make Sir Jeremy Swift marry Mama."

She opened her mouth, then closed it and seemed to ponder. I still stared at her, my lips firm with determination. She gazed at me assessingly, and a faint smile trembled at the corners of her mouth; it seemed as if she were about to laugh. "My dear, that would be something to see if it could be done! Sir Jeremy has resisted all his relatives' attempts to make him marry. But do you know . . ." Her smile grew wider. "I believe you could, if you set your mind to it. I really believe you could." Miss Angstead put her hands flat on her desk. "And I shall help you," she said.

I could have been knocked down with a feather—as Grimley, Mama's abigail, would say—when Miss Angstead announced that she would instruct me in the art of being in a decline. I am afraid I did not do credit to my scholarly reputation. I stared at her, my jaws agape, hands clutching and wrinkling my skirts.

"For goodness' sake, girl, close your mouth and sit up straight!" Miss Angstead said testily.

"B-but I, what is—I mean, I do *not* understand."

"I believe I said I would help you go into a decline." Miss Angstead smiled.

I wondered if the Headmistress had gone mad. I surveyed her carefully. She looked as she always did: somewhat untidy hair graying to white, large, intelligent brown eyes, a firm and competent mouth in a slim, lined face. She did not seem deranged in any way. Perhaps there was something more to be explained.

"I do not want to be pert, ma'am," I said cautiously, "but I wish you would explain to me what you mean."

"I will let you go home," she replied, and held

up her hand as I blushed and opened my mouth. "Not in disgrace, though your actions certainly do warrant it! But your motives are laudable, and I have a desire to see Sir Jeremy Swift . . . reformed." She clasped her hands together and looked at me in a satisfied manner.

"I still don't understand, Miss Angstead. Do you know Sir Jeremy? And," I reflected in some consternation, "if he needs to be reformed, I don't know if I want him for Mama."

Miss Angstead clicked her tongue. "My dear, all of us need to be reformed in some manner, some more or less than others. Yes, I am acquainted with him. We are somewhat related. It is the opinion of most of his family that he should end his bachelor ways—he is thirty-nine now, nearly forty."

I nodded. "That *is* old, isn't it?"

She raised her eyebrows at me but continued. "I think there would be little objection if he married a lady such as your mother."

I bristled. "Excuse me, Miss Angstead, but I would like to know what you mean by that!"

"My dear, I did not mean offense, but I must be blunt if we are going to enter into a plan of action. I am aware it is rumored your mother has had . . . ah, associations. If she has, she has also been discreet, and there is nothing at which anyone can point a finger. But she has two disadvantages. First, she is a widow with no male protection. Second, and worse, she is remarkably pretty and popular with men. That she has no male relative to protect her would not even be a disadvantage if she were not pretty—people do believe worse about handsome widows than plain. A mark in her favor is that she is Mrs. Canning, the widow of the third son of the Viscount Canning."

"She is a tradesman's daughter," I said, baring all. "*That* cannot be in her favor."

"True, but if I recall, your grandmother was of genteel birth. Also, your mother had the good taste to marry and follow your father, who distinguished himself under Wellington before he sacrificed his life for his country."

I had to admit that this last item was certainly a fine thing. But if Miss Angstead could be blunt, so could I. "But why my mother? There are probably more . . . acceptable . . . ladies, younger, too, who are available. Is there something wrong with him that other ladies do not like?"

The Headmistress smiled wryly. "Hardly. He has had caps set at him since he first came out on the town. As for more 'acceptable' ladies, as you put it, he has shown no lasting interest in any of them. His family has tried innumerable ways to draw certain eligible females to his attention—to no avail. But there is one tack no one has taken, and that is to encourage him to marry a lady in whom he is already interested."

"But he must have been interested in many ladies already!"

"To be sure he has," Miss Angstead said dryly, "but none so respectable as your mother." I was not sure how to take this but let it pass. She rubbed her hands together. "So! I shall help you look as if you are going into a decline, you will go home, recover your health, and work to make Sir

Jeremy marry your mother."

All of a sudden I felt less confident of my plans. After all, what could I, at seventeen, do in the wide world? I looked down at my clasped hands. "How . . . why do you think *I* can do this when you and his relatives cannot? I am not even sure I am equal to it."

Miss Angstead looked at me with a serious expression. "For all your years, you are intelligent, can face facts—however unpleasant—and are remarkably ingenious at inventing ways to accomplish your aims. Further, you have already been successful at bringing mere inclinations to a head; in fact, I must congratulate you on your first matchmaking." She smiled widely.

"Matchmaking? I haven't done any match-making. . . ." I thought of Miss Lauderdale's words when she took care of me. I hadn't bothered to puzzle over them then and had forgotten them since.

Miss Angstead seemed to read my thoughts. "Yes, Miss Lauderdale and the curate, Mr. Ainsley-Jones. It seems last Sunday brought him to a decision—"

"But I did not mean to bring them together!" I protested. "It was all an accident—I am very happy for them, to be sure—but I never had a thought to making Mr. Ainsley-Jones declare himself by giving up my dinner on Miss Standish!"

Miss Angstead tapped her foot impatiently. "As I was saying—"

I murmured apologetically.

She continued. "You have a talent for bringing matters to a head, whether intentionally or not."

Miss Angstead sat back and looked out the window into the misty afternoon scene. "I have often thought that there are some people who are catalysts for Providence; a sort of Philosopher's Stone of Fate. People whose very presence makes things happen. A situation may have all the elements for fortune or disaster, but nothing may occur until one such person enters the stage."

"And you think I am one of these . . . people?" I thought of the Wollstonecraft essays in the closet-library—which I understood by this time most people saw as radical—and reflected that perhaps Miss Angstead was more than a little eccentric. A perfect lady, of course, but not in the common way.

Miss Angstead returned her gaze to me and smiled. "You may not know this, but you are very good at making people reveal themselves. I realize this was not your intention last Sunday, but you showed clearly to me—and to Mr. Ainsley-Jones—the characters of Miss Lauderdale and Miss Standish.

"You were quite democratic in your illness, by the by. You became, er, ill on Miss Lauderdale as well. But Miss Lauderdale was in the line of fire, not inadvertently, but because she rushed to your aid. Meanwhile, Miss Standish shrieked her way into a fit of hysterics." Miss Angstead waved a hand in a dismissing gesture. "*She* had to be taken away and put to bed. Miss Lauderdale, with great fortitude, continued to care for you—much to the admiration of Mr. Ainsley-Jones. Who better for a future vicar's wife than a woman who could continue to care for others despite indignities to herself?" Miss Angstead gave a wry smile. "I am sure her calmness and self-possession in such a distasteful situation brought visions of Miss Lauderdale ministering to his future ailing parishioners."

"But I did not intend for any of that to happen," I protested again.

Miss Angstead stopped me with an upraised hand. "My dear, your actions were catalytic. Think of the things you have done so far and what has happened. You insist on being rain-drenched and constantly creep from the school grounds to steal apples. You do not think these are happy instances because you were punished for them. But for me, they were. They made me think that this school was becoming very unpleasant for you. I investigated the matter and became aware that gossip was rife in these halls—a condition I deplore. So you see, when you became ill I was not surprised. It simply fit the pattern. When I questioned you and you revealed your reasons, I found your mother was involved with Sir Jeremy.

"The result of your actions revealed to me the reliability of some of my schoolmistresses. You have also given me the opportunity to restore some measure of respectability to Sir Jeremy's life. It does not matter that your actions were inadvertent. Your nature is such that you cannot help but bring situations to a head. I expect that whatever happens when you return home, whatever has been obscure will become clear. If Sir Jeremy has serious intentions toward your mother, you will see that. If he does not, you will see that, too, and I hope you will endeavor to show him your mother is worthy of marriage."

I swallowed. I still did not see how she could have such confidence in me. But the important matter was that my mother be considered respectable again and that she not be gossiped about. I knew I would do all I could to bring that about.

Miss Angstead put her hands flat on the desk before her. "You will do it, if I help you, will you not?" she said with a sense of finality.

I looked straight into her wise eyes. "Yes, ma'am!" I said firmly, and then almost laughed, for I mentally snapped my fingers and thought: *That* for Mama's scruples!

"Good! Now, I will give you a white powder to put on your face in the morning—I will put a touch of green powder in it to make you look especially anaemic. . . ."

A few days later I was carried gently to my carriage by a strong and handsome young footman. My schoolmates gathered at the gates of the Seminary to watch me leave. My interestingly pale visage and fainting form was gazed upon with awe by the younger girls, and the older ones eyed my conveyance to the coach with envy. I waved a handkerchief to all of them, gazing at them with what I hoped were sad eyes, and committed the sight of them to my mind. I savored the memory of their admiring and envious faces for the whole of the trip home.

2

I arrived home, and Mama flew out of
the house, hurried down the steps, and wrenched
open the carriage door. "Georgia, my love! My
poor dear!" she exclaimed, searching me with
anxious eyes. She signaled the footman to carry
me into the house. I was brought to my bedroom and laid on the bed. Mama hovered over me
distractedly.

"Really, Mama, you needn't fuss. I will be better
in short order," I said faintly. "It's only anaemia.
Dr. Finchley said I was simply to have rest and eat
well, and I will recover." It was lucky I *had* stolen
those apples and eaten them all; combined with
my experience of ipecac, I had lost weight since
last I had seen Mama, and it showed. To make it
all the more impressive, Miss Angstead had

shown me how to dab a tiny amount of charcoal beneath my eyes to make them look a bit sunken.

Mama continued wringing her hands. "Yes, Miss Angstead wrote to me about it—so kind of her! *She* is of the opinion you have been over-taxing yourself with studying. And those girls! I have no doubt they are the ones behind this. I have been wondering since I left you at the school if you would be driven to distraction despite your brave, brave words! Miss Angstead was so kind as to give Dr. Finchley's remedy for this—red wine with each meal after breakfast, and I will order Cook to procure spinach, blackberries, and calf's liver every day."

Miss Angstead had not told me about the calf's liver. I despised calf's liver. But I could make do with the wine and blackberries and tolerate the spinach. I had a horrid thought then: What if, in the way of most remedies, these things were not taken separately but mixed together in some horrible potion? I believe I paled under my powder, for Mama exclaimed that she would leave me to rest after my tiring journey.

I faced my first meal at home with trepidation and quite lost my appetite: unpleasant but useful, for my picking at my food gave even more credence to my "illness." But to my relief, Cook had made up the liver in a delicious pasty filled with vegetables and spices, and I scarcely tasted the liver at all. I did not eat all of it, however. One must keep up appearances, I told myself.

It is a very tedious thing to be ill. Mama insisted on midday naps and breakfast in bed, and if it were not for novels from our library, I would have gone mad from ennui. When I first came home, I conscientiously powdered my face with Miss Angstead's pale green powder every day, but as soon as the boredom rose to an intolerable pitch, I judged it time to lessen the application. On days when I looked healthier, I ventured suggestions that a carriage ride might be beneficial. At first Mama was adamantly against it, but after a few days and upon a doctor's approval, I was given leave to go out, as long as I was adequately protected from the cold.

I soon left off the powder altogether, though sometimes I still applied the charcoal beneath the eyes. I ate more heartily than before; this was easy, for Cook had been instructed to make the most delectable dishes she could think of that contained either blackberries, spinach, or liver. She did so magnificently.

By the time Mama judged I was ready to dine belowstairs, I had begun to plan what I would do when I met Sir Jeremy. A good officer first assesses the enemy before plunging into the thick of battle. While Sir Jeremy was not exactly an "enemy," he was the object of my actions, and before I decided to do anything about him, I would see if he was worth it. I had not long to wait.

Mama had been too anxious about my health to host any parties at home, but as soon as she could see the blush of health return to my cheeks, she began to go to the opera and other events. I was glad of it; I suppose if I had been truly ill, I would have appreciated her efforts. Indeed, I was grateful for her concern, but because

I was perfectly healthy, I had to endure being fussed over by both Mama and her abigail, Grimley, which made me irritable and snappish. To make it worse, when I growled at them, they would only look at each other and shake their heads as if to say "Georgia is so ill, poor little one! She is not her usual self because of it."

Mama began to entertain more; that is to say, she invited guests to dinner more than she had done. Any number of admirers who came to visit offered posies. Mama delivered most of these flowers to my room. She said that the visitors brought them for me, but I was sure they brought them so as to get in Mama's good books rather than in concern for a girl just out of the school-room. After all, I believed most of them did not remember that she even had a daughter. I was sure of it when Mama apologetically presented me with a puzzle one of them had brought— something one would give to an infant rather than a seventeen-year-old young lady!

I was not surprised when I received a get-well present from Sir Jeremy—whether he meant good or ill toward Mama, I expected he would be desirous to remain in her good opinion. I *was* surprised (and secretly pleased) at his choice: a locket with a perfect miniature of Mama within. It showed a particular thoughtfulness on his part to consider what sort of gift would please me . . . or was it only a thoughtful cunning? If it was the latter, it certainly succeeded, for when Mama saw it, her eyes shone and she exclaimed over the gift, much moved.

I was even more determined to come down
when visitors called after this; Sir Jeremy seemed
to me a clever man—very clever—and I felt I
should find out if others of his ilk were keeping
company with my mother. Further, I did not feel
it proper she should keep company alone, with
only her abigail for protection.

I had support from a surprising quarter in this
respect. One day, when I heard that there were visitors belowstairs, I jumped out of bed, telling Grimley as I dressed that I would help Mama entertain
them. She stared at me fixedly for a minute, then
nodded briskly. "You do that, miss! I may be her
abigail and as I see it, part of my duties is to be at
her side, but this household has more to do in it
than one body can manage! You may be a young
lady, but it's a wise head you have on your shoulders, and it's better for your mother that one of her
kin look out for her, poor lady, than an abigail, however long I've been with your family! And that's a
long time, miss, *if* I may say so, seeing as how I
came to chaperone your mother straight from your
grandfather's house when she married your father!"
She gave another brisk and competent nod.

I stared at her for a moment, a bit awed. This
was the longest speech I had ever heard from her,
and apparently she was working under powerful
emotion, for her long nose quivered, her pale blue
eyes turned a steely grey, and her thin lips almost
disappeared as she gripped them together in a
determined frown.

I went to her and took her hand, pressing it.
"You may be sure, Miss Grimley, I shall do all that

I ought. And I am grateful for all you have done for us, too!"

Grimley's thin cheeks grew pink. "Ah, be off with you, then! I suppose I'm well enough, thank you!" she said gruffly.

I skipped to the door, but before I left the room I turned back to the abigail. "You know, Grimley, I mean to have Mama respectably married."

She looked at me and shook her head. "Lord help me if I can see how you will. But I'll not stand in your way if you can!"

In general, the company my mother kept seemed refined. Before I was permitted downstairs, I would tiptoe quietly from my room and peer between the balusters at Mama's visitors. They appeared, from the descriptions Emily had related to me, to be mostly dandies who must have deemed it fashionable to be at Mama's feet. I soon discounted them as serious contenders for Mama's favors; they were interested only in what was fashionable and displaying various affectations such as lisps, over-large buttons, and eye-searing waistcoats. Mama took them as seriously as I did—not very—for she often humorously rolled her eyes heavenward after they left.

More serious predators were the Corinthians; addicted to sporting activities, they were certainly fine figures of men. Their clothes were relatively plain but so well cut that one couldn't help but notice the natural breadth of their shoulders or their well-muscled legs. I recalled Mama once saying that Father had been one of this group, and this made me feel uneasy. She would be more susceptible to these men than the dandies.

I found Sir Jeremy Swift was one as well. Indeed, as a man of nearly forty (and quite elderly, I thought, for he was starting to become grey at the temples), Sir Jeremy was an example par excellence to the younger men of the set. He was tall, large boned, and well muscled, and as I listened from my spot on the stairs, I gathered that he excelled at boxing, was a fine horseman, and was equally good with swords or pistols.

As it turned out, I did not meet him at dinner as Mama had planned. I saw him not long after breakfast one morning.

Mother usually took a light repast of toast and chocolate in her room so was not yet downstairs. I had already taken mine and was curled up on a big chair by the fireplace, reading Plato's *Apologia* when Sir Jeremy was escorted into the parlour. I imagine Bartley, our butler, did not know I was there, so when Sir Jeremy walked into the room unannounced, I started and dropped my book.

He turned sharply at the sound and saw me. I hurriedly sat up properly and smoothed my skirts, then remembered I had dropped my book and bent to retrieve it. But he was there before me, picked it up, and handed it to me. "How do you do, Miss Canning. Since I caused you to drop your book, it is only right that I retrieve it for you, is it not?" He smiled.

I could see why Mama found him attractive. He was as I remembered him: black hair greying at the temples, uncompromising lines around his mouth, penetrating grey eyes, swarthy skin. But when he smiled his slightly crooked smile he grew young, for those steely eyes lit up with all the laughter of a child just venturing out into the world, inviting one to come along for sheer enjoyment. He reminded me of someone, but I could not remember who it was. I thought perhaps it was Miss Angstead since they were related but somehow was not satisfied with the answer. I could not help smiling back, but I forced myself to remember that I was going to survey his character with a keen and strict eye; after all, a man may have kindly laughter in his eyes but be an irresponsible rake.

"I thank you, sir," I said. I opened the book to smooth back any rumpled pages.

His eye caught the title. "Plato! You are quite a scholar, then. Have you read all of his works?"

"No, I have not. The library here only has a few books like this in it, and the school I go to . . . well, it is a young ladies' seminary, and Plato and Cicero are not deemed necessary to a young lady's education," I said with a touch of asperity. Perhaps he thought me a little pert, for a crease appeared between his brows and he frowned slightly. Much do I care! I thought to myself.

"A bluestocking, are you? You believe all young ladies should have a classical education?"

"Well, of course!" I replied, nettled at his mocking tone.

"All young ladies being as intelligent and bent on being a scholar as you are, of course," he con-

tinued casually. He flicked a nonexistent speck of
dust from his lapel.

I really did not know of any other girl who read
the works I did, and the idea of someone like
Emily Possett bending her powers on a passage
from Marcus Aurelius was ludicrous. I opened my
mouth, then shut it, not wanting to resemble a
fish. I looked at him suspiciously. "You aren't a
barrister, are you?" I asked.

He laughed. "No—" But he said no more, for
the door opened suddenly, and Mama floated
through.

A change came over Sir Jeremy: the harsh
lines of his face softened, and a warm and tender
light came into his eyes as he met those of my
mother's. "Celia!" he exclaimed.

"Dear Jeremy!" cried Mama, extending her hand,
her eyes full of love. She saw me fidgeting a bit
behind him, clutching my book. "And Georgia, my
love! I see you two have met. How delightful!
Ah, Jeremy, is she not a dear girl? She is becoming
a most exceptional young lady." She bent and
kissed my cheek.

I smiled at her. "I hope I will, Mama."

"Hardly more so than her exceptional mama."
Sir Jeremy smiled.

"Oh, Jeremy!" chided Mama, lightly slapping
the hand that held hers still. "Of course she will
be!" She lifted eyes brimful of laughter to his.

It was then my heart dropped to the bottom of
my shoes. I saw, suddenly, of whom it was that
Sir Jeremy reminded me. Mama's sparkling sky
blue eyes, as she laughingly raised them to Sir

Jeremy's, were filled with the same childlike wonder of the world as his, now looking into hers. It seemed almost as if with each glance they gave each other, they shared a delightful secret that no one else—poor things!—could understand. I remembered vaguely how it was said in the church service that when a man and a woman married, they "became one flesh." I looked at Mama and Sir Jeremy and thought they were one soul.

I never felt more alone in my life than I did in that moment. It never occurred to me, when I first resolved to have Mama become married and respectable, that she might be lost to me. Of course, I reminded myself stoutly, it would happen eventually, one day when I became a schoolmistress—but I could not deny that another route I had envisioned for myself was one of standing by and caring for Mama in her old age. I wondered morosely if she would miss me when I would be away with my young charges.

I think I must have turned pale, for Mama was at once upon me, fussing. Sir Jeremy came to my rescue. "Perhaps she would feel better if she accompanied us on our morning ride. I would be glad of your company, Miss Canning," he said kindly.

I needed to be alone to think about what I might actually accomplish if I helped Mama and Sir Jeremy marry. So I smiled slightly and thanked him, saying that I did indeed feel tired and needed to rest.

Mama was inclined to stay with me, but I

insisted I was quite all right and that she go out. Sir Jeremy looked concerned, too, but I smiled reassuringly at him and bade them enjoy their ride.

After they left, I neither rested nor was left alone to think. Bartley, perhaps warned that I was in the parlour, announced my next visitor. "Lord Lucas Ashcombe!"

I sighed in annoyance. Bartley was an old and faithful retainer, but because he *was* very old, he had a habit of forgetting occasionally when one went out and when one was not at home to visitors. Mama did not want to dismiss him because it would hurt him, and I agreed, but it did make things awkward sometimes. As it did now. Bartley merely smiled and nodded at me when he saw me in the parlour. He seemed to forget the proprieties where I was concerned, for the butler still thought of me as a little child rather than a grown young lady. As a result, he allowed Lord Ashcombe in and did not call for a maid to chaperone me. Fortunately Bartley also forgot to close the door.

One of Mama's admirers, Lord Ashcombe was a handsome young man, and that was the problem— he was young. Calf-love, said Mama, feeling sorry for him, for it was clear that at three-and-twenty years, he was in love for the first time. To repulse him outright would be the cruelest thing imaginable, she declared. I thought to repulse him outright would probably be the most *sensible* thing imaginable. However much Mama treated him like the boy she perceived him to be or gently snubbed him from time to time, he persisted in writing silly poems and dogging her steps whenever he saw her.

Were it not for the fact he was too young for Mama—why, she could almost be *his* mother!—I would have liked him well enough. Indeed, when I first saw him, I knew him to be far more handsome than Sir Jeremy. Mama did not agree with this, but I remembered that as one grew older, one's eyesight was not always very acute and saw that this was perhaps the root of her opinion.

There was nothing wrong with *my* eyesight, however. Lord Ashcombe had curling, true black hair—so black it shone blue in the sunlight—and his profile was just enough short of classical to be interesting. The planes of his face were lean and his chin stubborn, but his lips could curl in the most delightful smile. He had large, sleepy violet eyes fringed with lashes a girl would envy and a way of looking at one that made one shiver—or perhaps that was only me, for Mama seemed unaffected by it. She often laughed at him for it, saying he did a good imitation of Byron's Corsair. He was tall and looked graceful, but I found somewhat to my chagrin that he had not yet totally outgrown a certain awkwardness. I will confess I had a *tendre* for him, but it was short-lived; there is nothing like a young man making a fool of himself to make a girl fall out of her infatuation with him.

And so it was with poor Lord Ashcombe; anyone could see that he was so much younger than the rest of Mama's admirers and that she did not consider him seriously. But I deduced from one of the poems he wrote that her kindly condescension only spurred him to greater efforts, for he saw her as "a princess pure/whose eyes doth hold distant allure" and something about unmindful disdain prompting him to display no pain when he went out to conquer exotic plains. He had finished Oxford, and I thought that august institution should have made him a better poet, but perhaps these were his first rhymes and he only needed practice to become better.

He did have a somewhat dramatic air about him. As Bartley held open the door, Lord Ashcombe seemed almost to leap into the parlour, and at once he started to declaim: "Oh, Celia of the gold hair/Thou sinketh me into deep despair—"

"I'm sorry, but my mother is not here," I cut in bluntly, then giggled because I had unintentionally half rhymed him. He turned to find me sitting on the chair by the fireplace, and he flushed all the way up to his ears.

"I was told that *Mrs*. Canning was here," he said stiffly, nervously passing the posy he had brought from his right hand to his left and back again.

"Please do sit down, Lord Ashcombe. I am sorry for the mistake, but Bartley has been with us for so many years and is becoming quite forgetful. I am sure he meant *Miss* Canning and did not mean to mislead you. Would you like some refreshment?" I asked.

My conciliatory tone seemed to placate him somewhat, for though he looked at me suspiciously, he said: "Yes, thank you, Miss Canning, I would like some. This damn—dashed poetry writing does make one feel rather dry. Popped it off before I came, you know. Meant to present it to your mother; thought *she'd* appreciate it." He glowered at me as if to say "even if *you* do not."

I rang for tea and biscuits. "Alas, she has gone out for a carriage ride. You have missed her by half an hour. Sir Jeremy Swift came at eleven for her."

"Him!" uttered Lord Ashcombe in accents of extreme loathing. He jumped up from his chair and paced the room like a caged tiger, and if he had had a tail, I am sure he would have lashed it. "That a—a libertine like Swift dare touch even the hem of her gown!"

I knew a moment of unease at these words but on reflection saw it was jealousy on his part. Sir Jeremy was of the Corinthian set; one glance at Lord Ashcombe's attire told me that he aspired to be one of them. I noticed, too, that his neckcloth was tied in a very similar style to Sir Jeremy's. How humiliating it must have been for his lordship to find his example also to be his rival!

I felt I should treat Lord Ashcombe as kindly as possible, for I had decided that whatever Sir Jeremy's intentions, he did seem to have at least a strong affection for Mama and did not seem to be the sort to give up lightly what he had. It might be a hard blow for Lord Ashcombe if Mama did marry Sir Jeremy.

"I had not heard that Sir Jeremy was a libertine. Is he so very loose in his morals?" I asked.

"Mistresses!" Lord Ashcombe said darkly. "For years!"

"But don't most men have them?" I felt I should have been shocked at the mention of such a thing, but the topic was too intriguing for me to leave alone.

He puffed out his chest a little. "Well, when one is a man of the town, one does get about, you know. But one doesn't flaunt—I mean to say—" He stopped and eyed me sternly. "What business does a schoolgirl chit like you have asking questions about mistresses?"

"Why, you were the one who brought it up!"

"Well, you needn't take one up so!" he said testily. "I may have brought it up, but you still shouldn't be asking questions about them! You shouldn't even pretend to know what they are!"

"You're out there!" I retorted. "I do know what they are, so I don't have to pretend!"

"Learned about them from the servants, eh?" He did a good imitation of a Byronic sneer.

"Not at all." I smiled sweetly. "Mama told me."

He looked daunted at this but recovered, scowling. "It's Swift's dashed influence, no doubt! Trying to make that goddess stoop to his level! Preying on a defenseless widow—I'd like to see him try! He will have me to answer to, you may be sure!"

"I am sure that will not be necessary," I said coolly. I resented his trying to usurp my role as Mama's protector. "Who are you, after all, to claim responsibility for Mama's welfare?"

He regarded me with a fiery eye. "*I* mean to *marry* her, though Sir Jeremy may not!"

I wanted to burst out laughing at that, and I know my face grew warm with the effort not to. I managed to say brightly, with only a slight tremor: "Oh, how delightful! That means you shall be my new papa!"

Lord Ashcombe's foot seemed to catch on the rug and effectively stopped his pacing as he turned to stare at me in pop-eyed horror. I don't know if he caught hold of the chair back to support himself or to keep from tripping farther on the rug. "I—I hadn't thought—you wouldn't— of course—Good God!" he uttered in a revulsed voice. Apparently Mama had not brought this aspect of her life to his attention.

I looked meltingly into his eyes. "Wouldn't you *like* to be my new papa?" I said with sweet wistfulness.

He stared back at me for a long moment with the expression of a hunted deer, then seemed to recover. "You will be going back to your school shortly, won't you?" he said half-hopefully.

I looked down at my hands clasped on my lap and glanced up through my lashes. "Oh, I expect not. I was sent home because I have overdone myself with studying. I am nearly eighteen now, so I suppose by the time I fully recover, it will be too late to go back. I know I can keep up with my studies at home—indeed, the headmistress says I am far above the oldest students in her school even now. Although I daresay she is merely being kind in saying so." I cast down my eyes modestly.

Silence reigned for the next few minutes while Lord Ashcombe digested all this. Bartley entered with the tea and biscuits, and I became busy pouring the hot liquid into Mama's dainty teacups. I stole a look at my lord's face after I gave him a cup, and though I managed not to laugh aloud, my shoulders shook so much that I hastily set down my own cup before I spilled any tea. His starting eyes had earlier been expressive of horror when he realized he would be a father upon marriage with Mama. Now his eloquently hangdog look showed that even if he could entertain *that* thought, being saddled with a seventeen-year-old girl at the tender age of three-and-twenty was too much to be borne. By the time he looked up at me again, I had myself sufficiently under control to smile demurely at him.

A thought seemed to strike him, and he said, faint but pursuing: "I know! You like the country, don't you? Well, I have a respectable estate you could stay at until it is time for you to be presented." His voice rose questioningly at the end, as if he were cautiously offering a bone to a growling dog.

I shook my head. "Oh, but I adore London! And Mama would never consent to having us parted, especially after my illness."

His face fell again into such morose dejection that I could stand it no longer. I tried to stifle my laugh behind my hand but only ended up snorting in a very unladylike way, which brought his eyes sharply to my face.

"Why, you—!" he cried.

"Oh, goodness!" I moaned. "Your f-face! I have never s-seen anyone more d-dejected at the thought of marrying Mama!" I clutched my stomach with one hand, gripped the arm of my chair with the other, and gasped with laughter, kicking the rug with my feet.

His face had frozen at my first snort of laughter, but the corners of his mouth trembled upward slightly. "Oh, no! Not at marrying your mama! It was just the terror of someday presenting to all and sundry a ramshackle minx like you! My *God*," he said in tones of horror, "that *would* be devastating!"

I managed to grab a pillow from behind me for support, and at this I let go of another wail of muffled laughter. His own shout of laughter brought me out for air, but when I caught his eye, we both collapsed again.

It was in this state that Mama and Sir Jeremy came upon us. Mama entered first, and at the same time Lord Ashcombe and I looked at her and then glanced at each other. Again we started to laugh but tried desperately to stifle it.

Mama beamed at us. "So nice to see young people enjoying themselves, although I can hardly see what it is about me to set you two off laughing—is my hat askew?"

I noticed that Lord Ashcombe did not wince at Mama's phrase "young people" but merely grinned at her in a mischievous way and looked at me, daring me to tell her. Though Mama was oblivious of his difference in attitude, Sir Jeremy seemed to notice a change, for he raised his eyebrows at his lordship's unbesotted face and then transferred his keen gaze to me. I smiled at him in limpid innocence and turned to Mama.

"I don't mean to be impertinent, Mama, but I don't think we can compose ourselves enough to say right now— I assure you, you look quite lovely, and we were not laughing at you at all."

Mama and Sir Jeremy sat down and partook of the tea that was left—quite a bit, as Lord Ashcombe and I had been too busy laughing to eat and drink.

I think, of all the calls Mama and I have had from gentlemen, this was the most comfortable. We chatted of this and that, all at ease; Lord Ashcombe had lost his awkwardness around Mama simply because he had suddenly lost his infatuation for her. Indeed, he handed her the posy he brought with all the respect that could be given to an elderly lady in failing health—and joked and laughed for all the world as if he were sitting at home. Sir Jeremy was the only one who did not enter into the conversation much, but he seemed to survey us all in amused benevolence.

Lord Ashcombe left soon, as he had promised to squire his sisters to the shops—this he reported with a slightly disgusted look that disappeared when he saw it was going to set me off again. He took his leave, bowing to Mama and then to me with a laugh in his eye.

"Well, I must say, Lord Ashcombe was certainly less impetuous in manner than usual!" exclaimed Mama. "Not, of course, that he isn't a dear, good boy, but so pressing in his attentions! But today— why, if I did not know I am not a day over six-and-thirty, I would have thought he believed me near my dotage!" She gave a trill of laughter. "And it is just as well if he did, poor boy!"

"You may have your daughter to thank for that, I think," said Sir Jeremy, amused.

Mama looked at me, surprised. "Georgia? But, my dear, she is not yet eighteen! That is not to say she is not a lovely girl, but . . . Oh, Jeremy, do you think it is true? Lord Ashcombe for my dear, dear girl! Oh, Georgia, I know you are still young yet, but it would be everything I could wish for!"

"Mama, *please!*" I said, blushing furiously. "It is not like that at all, I assure you! Indeed, he changed in attitude because of what we were laughing about when you and Sir Jeremy came in. He was striking one of his Byronic poses, saying that *he* would marry you if"—I cast a surreptitious glance at Sir Jeremy—"no one else would." Mama looked taken aback at this and opened her mouth to comment, but I rushed on. "He was very serious in offering you protection. But I brought to his attention the fact that I would then become his daughter, and he looked so despondent about it, I laughed, and so did he." Mama again looked as if she would say something but was interrupted by Sir Jeremy's shout of laughter.

"Indeed! A daunting prospect! I do not doubt he quailed at the thought of acquiring you as a daughter! It puts me in a quake even to think of it!" he said, chuckling.

"Now, really, Jeremy! Georgia is an exceptional girl, a wonderful daughter!" Mama protested.

"I'll agree with the exceptional, and add 'a handful' to it as well! What a wonderful way of ridding you of your suitors, Celia! Tell me, Miss

Georgia, do you plan to use this tactic on the rest of your mother's admirers?"

"Jeremy! This is most improper!" Mama exclaimed faintly.

I was not sure whether I felt indignant or amused, but the image of dandies fleeing the house in droves came to me, and I nearly laughed. I fixed Sir Jeremy with a challenging eye and said: "Why not, if it will work?"

He returned a quizzical look. "And if not all of them are scared away? What then?"

I stood up to ring for the refreshments to be taken away. "Why, the one left, I suppose, will have to become my papa!" I retorted pertly, curtsied, and skipped out of the room.

3

I sustained only a light lecture from Mama that afternoon for my pertness toward Sir Jeremy; she seemed to be thinking of Lord Ashcombe's change of heart.

"And I must say, Georgia, it was also not very well mannered of you to make fun of Lord Ashcombe, either, although he did take it in good part. Such a good-natured young man! And so eligible! So particular in his attentions to you!"

I blushed. I felt more abashed by this than by any lecture Mama could give me. "I beg to differ, Mama. If we seemed to be . . . be friendly with each other, it is only because we had laughed together before you came into the parlour. I am sure his lordship has no feelings toward me at all, other than simple civility. After all, he has been in love with you for ages—how could he switch his affections so suddenly to me?"

Mama waved a dismissing hand. "Calf-love! And why should he not acquire a *tendre* for you? You are much nearer his age, and you are quite a lovely young lady. I have always thought you have a look of your dear papa—quite a handsome man—although Sir Jeremy said yesterday you are growing to look much like myself, which I cannot quite see as an advantage, for I have always thought my nose a trifle too short."

I resisted an urge to run upstairs and look in the mirror; I felt gratified that Sir Jeremy saw in me a resemblance to Mama, for I had always thought her the most beautiful lady I had ever seen.

Mama sighed. "'Tis true you are but seventeen, but that is not so *very* young. . . ."

"That is precisely it," I said instantly. "We are both too young. Why, only think, Mama! Lord Ashcombe fell out of his infatuation with you in less than a half hour! Even if he did have a *tendre* for me—which he does not, I assure you—just think how quickly he would transfer his affections to another!"

Mama's brow furrowed for a moment, then cleared. "Youth! It is hardly the calf-love it was for me, after all. We shall see!"

In vain I argued, for Mama literally laughed it off, saying I needn't be so modest, sly minx, indeed she was pleased I had an admirer already. It was hard to bring Mama around to see the folly of her notions. She always seemed to slip through one's grasp like a ball of grease between the fingers. I gave it up. Time would show her I was right when Lord Ashcombe's visits grew fewer.

As it was, Lord Ashcombe did not come to call as often as he was used to, but he still was a regular caller. "After all," he remarked, "can't insult your mama by cutting her acquaintance, now, can I? Besides, there's always jolly good company here, better than at home. Get to know all the Corinthians!"

"Yes, but Mama has come to think . . ." I blushed. "She is thinking that your attentions are getting most particular. . . ."

Lord Ashcombe's ears became a little pink, but he said: "Can't think I'm still in love with her! I haven't written a sonnet in weeks! Oh, I might bring a posy for her once in a while but I give one to you, too."

"Well, that's just it!" I retorted. "What is she to think when you start giving *me* flowers when you haven't before?"

The ears took on a bright red color, pushing the pink to his cheeks. A hunted look crept into his eyes. "But, but you've just returned from school! She can't think—"

"Oh, yes, she can! Mama is very fond of me, and I know she wishes to establish me creditably—and thinks to have me married well. And if you think, my lord, that you are not one of the most eligible bachelors in London, your modesty overcomes your good sense!"

He eyed me warily. "*You* haven't thought that I—"

"No, I have not!" I interrupted crossly. I sighed

and sipped my tea, thinking of my plans for Mama, which were getting more tangled by the minute. "How things do get complicated!" I exclaimed. "Instead of getting Mama interested in her own marriage, she is now thinking of mine!"

"Is your mama to be married? I don't think I have read anything in the *Gazette* of it."

"And you are not like to. Sir Jeremy has asked her to marry him, but she has refused him."

"Well! Never thought it of him—he's been a confirmed bachelor as far as the ton is concerned these last ten years. Except to his female relatives, of course. Something about female relatives—keep egging a man on to marriage, will he, nil he! I mean, look at me! Only three-and-twenty and m'mater's already baiting the parson's mousetrap!"

I grinned at this but sympathized, for I fully understood the pressures one's mother could put on one. I said: "Yes, Miss Angstead at the seminary seemed very determined that Sir Jeremy marry, although I suppose at forty he has less of an excuse than you do for being a bachelor."

He smiled back. "Angstead! Met her once at Mater's. A bit on the eccentric side, running a school when she could just as well be living in Town. She has an eye, though, that can cut you in half at twenty paces. Remarkable woman, but I'm glad she's not *my* aunt!" he said carelessly.

"Aunt!" I squeaked, indignant. "Do you mean to tell me she is Sir Jeremy's *aunt*?"

"Well, yes! Everyone knows that! She's been scheming with her sisters for ages, trying to get Sir Jeremy leg-shackled."

Well! I thought to myself. And I thought I was devious with all my schemes for getting home! But I reflected on Lord Ashcombe's words and thought perhaps Miss Angstead had been feeling as desperate to get Sir Jeremy married as I was for Mama. Why else would she resort to using a mere schoolgirl like myself?

"Mere" was in the right of it, too! I had been home for months now, but I was still no closer to making Mama accept Sir Jeremy's offer of marriage. To be sure, I would from time to time wistfully mention in Mama's presence how nice it would be to have a papa, but she would only look at me sadly and murmur that she had done the best she could. I could not continue my complaints then, for I knew how difficult her life had been in the past, and guilt overcame my ambitions.

I made the mistake once of voicing my wish to Mama in the hearing of Sir Jeremy. I suppose—no, I know—I was too bold; I was becoming frustrated at how stagnant my plans for Mama and Sir Jeremy had become, and I resorted to unfair tactics. Sir Jeremy and I had become friends after our first altercation, and I forgot at times that he was older than I; you may take from this that I had concluded he was well enough to be Mama's husband and my new father. I would be pert to him in a funning sort of way, but I suppose I would sometimes overstep what was proper. Mama was quick to take me up on it, for she often exclaimed that no daughter of hers was going to give cause for scandal—although how a bit of pertness would cause *that* was quite beyond my imagination.

I must admit I had not been in a very good mood that day, for I had been brooding about the tangled web of my plans. Sir Jeremy was in a teasing mood with Mama, twitting her on her new hat, which sported an alarming number of papier-mâché cherries on it.

"You will set a new fashion, Celia. Yours will be the only bonnet with sparrows on it," he said.

"What can you be talking of? This hat has cherries, not birds!" exclaimed Mama. She was wearing a charming robe-dress with cerise piping that exactly matched the hat. She held out the hat for him to see.

Sir Jeremy looked at her solemnly and tapped a false cherry with his finger. "Once you step outside, birds from all around London will spy your bonnet, and think it a feast laid out for their benefit."

"Nonsense!"

"Not at all. I can see it clearly: hundreds of sparrows upon your hat, and you so covered with their wings, you will seem an angel." His face was still serious, but the glance he cast at me twinkled.

"I would be overwhelmed with their weight, rather, and sustain a serious injury!" Mama replied tartly, but the corners of her mouth quivered upward briefly.

"No, no!" said Sir Jeremy. "Each one would seize an ornament and try to fly off with it. You would need to keep your bonnet firmly tied, of course, but you would feel as light as a . . . er, feather."

I groaned and rolled my eyes. Once Mama and

Sir Jeremy got started on their nonsense, nothing
stopped them. They were as bad as children. At
first I was amused by their banter. These days I
felt more irritated than not. I wistfully eyed the
new book I had laid down on a side table when
Bartley had announced Sir Jeremy. Sophocles was
more to my mood than their absurdity.

"It is far more likely I should strangle!" retorted
Mama.

Sir Jeremy picked up the hat and eyed the long
wide ribbon that served as a tie for it. "You are
right. It is a dangerous bonnet. Let us discard it."
He tossed it over the back of the sofa.

"Jeremy, you odious, odious man!" cried Mama,
belatedly trying to catch it. "My new bonnet! You
will ruin it! I cannot buy another such, for it was
made to order for me!" She leaned as decorously
as she could over the back of the sofa, apparently
trying to snag some portion of the bonnet with a
finger.

"Marry me, and I will buy you all the bonnets
you could wish for, all made to order." Sir Jeremy
caught her other hand and held it firmly. Mama
turned to him, blushing, and lightly tapped his
restraining grip.

"As if I would marry anyone for such a reason!"
she returned.

"And why not, Mama?" I interjected. "Think of
all the bonnets you could have. You might as well
marry him for that reason as any other." I started
out speaking in a funning manner, but somehow—
perhaps it was my discontent revealing itself—that
last sentence came out sounding quite sarcastic.

Sir Jeremy's lips twitched appreciatively, but Mama did not find it amusing in the least.

She eyed me with a steely look and indicated that I should step out of the room. She usually only needed to take me out of the room and look at me for a minute for me to apologize. But this time I stared right back at her, wanting, somehow, in my frustration to do battle with something or someone, and since Mama was there, it might just as well be she.

"Well, my dear," she said coolly. "Liveliness is all very well, but you are getting a bit forward, are you not? I am surprised you have not yet learned that impertinence can only bring disgust into the feelings of a gentleman when he encounters it in a young girl. Perhaps I should send you back to Miss Angstead's after all." She looked at me and crossed her arms, tapping her fingers on her cheek in a thoughtful manner.

Fear clutched at me at this certain ruination of my plans, and anger wrestled it. Another stick thrust in my spokes! "Not," I said flippantly, "that there are any men there to set me straight if that is so."

Mama's mouth tightened, but she remarked in an even more cool tone: "And impertinence toward one's elders is even more disgusting. It seems you have not learned much at all at Miss Angstead's, have you?"

Wretchedness at Mama's rebuke combined with self-pitying anger overcame any caution I had. I had always been proud of my learning, and though I had made up with Sir Jeremy, his

suggestion that I had not really learned my Plato
still rankled. And here was Mama, once proud of
my accomplishments, now saying I had learned
nothing while at school! I clenched my teeth and
glared at Mama. "I have learned—academics! But
how do you suppose I am going to learn how to
get on with anything else but books! I suppose if I
had a *father,* I might have—"

I stopped in horror at what I was saying, for I
looked at Mama's wretched and stricken face, and
remorse overcame me at my thoughtless, stupid
words; how could I say such things when I knew
in my very heart of hearts that whatever Mama
had done was done in the best way she could and
for my benefit? I clapped my hands over my
mouth and turned away, saying: "I am sorry,
Mama, very sorry. I did not mean to say that, it
was wrong of me. I know you do what's best for
me, it's just that—that . . ." I could not reveal my
frustrated plans to her; indeed, I felt there was no
one I could discuss them with, so I said, "I've felt
so tired lately and irritable for no reason I can
think of. I know that does not excuse me, but
sometimes it overcomes me, and I am simply not
aware of what I am saying. The most stupid
things, too!" I looked up, about to turn around to
her again, and caught sight of the door, so very
slightly ajar. I could see Sir Jeremy's profile
through the doorway, and though he did not see
me, I realized by his arrested expression that he
had probably heard what I had said. No doubt my
voice had risen as I became excited. I turned
quickly back to Mama, leaning against the door

so that it shut gently. My red face probably convinced her of my very real remorse, and she extended her hand to mine.

"Apology accepted," she said, and kissed my cheek. "Perhaps it is your anaemia coming back."

I looked at her and saw that sad look again and wished I had never opened my mouth today, that I could take the words back. But of course what was done was done. I stared at my shoes and at my hands wringing each other.

"Now, now!" said Mama, smiling. "It's not as bad as all that! Come! Let's go back to Sir Jeremy, shall we?"

Perhaps I was mistaken, but it seemed from then on that Sir Jeremy became more . . . well, "paternal" toward me. He seemed to take more of an interest in my studies, brought me books, admonished me on taking better care of myself, teasing me that I was growing to look just like Mama. I was not sure whether Mama noticed this or not, but it did seem that whenever Sir Jeremy took my attention from her, a look of relief flickered over her face and then was gone. I felt a little hurt but supposed that perhaps since I had been at school for most of the years past, Mama was not used to having me at home at all hours. Indeed, I believe I was rather a burden on Mama, though she would never say so or even think it. After all, it is not an easy thing for a lone woman to raise a child, and to have to deal with a cantankerous and supposedly sickly one is probably worse.

While I was not really sickly, I was certainly at least cantankerous. I was bored when I was not at my studies. A young lady lives a restricted life in London. If I wished to go to the shops, I had to have a maid or a groom go with me, though this was seldom, as we had few servants. I could not go riding in London as freely as I could in the country around Bath for the same reason, and while there were diversions scheduled for the members of Miss Angstead's Seminary, there were few at home for me. That is not to say that Mama did not do her best to take me out to see the sights in London: she did. But our excursions were more likely than not to be made tedious (for me, at least) by the number of Mama's acquaintances (mostly male) who would catch sight of her and follow along like so many dogs after a pastry cart.

I think I would have given up all my plans and died from sheer ennui if it had not been for Lord Ashcombe. I *had* given up all efforts to convince Mama that he had no interest in me. Her love and hopes for me were such that they blinded her, I think, to any thought except the one that any young man who came to know me could not help but fall in love with me. While I was gratified that Mama thought so highly of me, I could not help but feel embarrassed that she had "set her cap" in the most obvious way at Lord Ashcombe on my behalf.

I think it would have embarrassed Lord Ashcombe as well if we had not talked of this between us and made it clear that neither one had any interests in the other, much less marriage. "After all," said his lordship, who appeared at our door one day just after Mama had gone out, "you're not much more than a schoolgirl, not yet Out, and I'm *just* out—of Oxford, that is. Been on the town in between terms, you know. Bet you a guinea you wouldn't want to get tied up in a church before you got a little Town bronze, eh?" I had persuaded him to stay for a bit, for I was bored. He had hesitated, but then entered the parlour, careful to keep the door ajar.

"Oh, no!" I exclaimed. "Why, there are all sorts of things I have not seen yet! The Tower of London! The British Exchange! Madame Tussaud's Waxworks!"

Lord Ashcombe looked taken aback. "Didn't precisely mean those sorts of things. What I meant was, well, balls, routs, dinners: having an introduction to the ton, learning how to get on, et cetera. Can't think you'd be getting to know the ton at the British Exchange! Full of cits and mushrooms! Not that that's bad, but you don't find people like that at ton parties!"

"Bah! Parties!" I wrinkled my nose. "Mama has them all the time here, or used to. They must be the most tedious things imaginable! And all the work which goes into them! It takes ever so many servants to set one up, and afterward, why, you have to hire even more to clean it up!"

He snorted and tossed a lock of hair from his forehead—just like a horse, I thought. "Which just goes to show what you know about them!" he retorted. "Why, you don't go gadding about with

servants when you are at a party! You don't even
think of them! It's different when you are invited
to one—you dance, talk with people, drink ratafia
or champagne, and all that. Servants!" he scoffed.
He glanced at me and relented. "Of course, I suppose you can't help just knowing about servants,
since you're barely out of the schoolroom."

"Well, why shouldn't I think of the servants?"
I argued, not wanting to be bested. I felt annoyed
at still being called a schoolgirl. I *was* seventeen,
after all, and Mama had married when she was
eighteen. "It *is* a bother to them and having to
direct them to do the thing properly! Why should
they suffer for the frivolities of others?" I concluded
nobly.

He eyed me disgustedly. "Because they are
hired to clean up. Besides, if people weren't so
frivolous as to have parties, there wouldn't be
any vails to earn or work for them to do, and if
there wasn't any work to do, they'd be out in the
streets starving because they wouldn't have
jobs!"

I pondered this, wanting to find a chink in his
logic, but I could not. I sighed. "I suppose you are
right. It seems I do *not* know much about society
at all. All I know about the world is what I've read
from books and from Emily Possett. She hears all
about the ton, and gossips, you know."

He shook his head. "Won't do. Oh, books are
well enough—have 'em at Oxford, you know. In
fact I—" He stopped dead and looked at me warily.
"And you can't very well get to know about the
world from a dashed gossip!" he continued.

"'In fact you' what?" I asked, curious.

"Did I say that?" Lord Ashcombe said, looking around as if there had been someone else in the room who could have.

"Yes, silly! Now, what were you going to say?" I teased.

"Nothing important at all."

"Now, let's see. It has to do with books. You have them at Oxford." I glanced mischievously at his harassed face. "In fact you . . ." I allowed a look of mock horror to dawn on my face. "Oh, Lord Ashcombe! Could it be . . . could it be that you actually . . . *like* books? Could it be that you are even—" I raised my hand to my forehead. "Bookish?" I was well aware that to be studious for a girl was certainly not the thing, but I did not fully realize that this extended to young men as well.

"Well, I—" he began.

"Oh, horror! Alack! Alas! That I have harbored an unfashionably bookish man in our house!" I clutched at my heart as if I were on the verge of palpitations. I received a pillow in my face for my pains. I peered over it at him, laughing.

He was grinning wryly. "Oh, stubble it! If you had been on the town like I have, you'd know it's not something you'd want bruited about, unless you were looking to be a clergyman for the rest of your life. Which I am not! And it's not fashionable, for another."

"I am surprised that should be a consideration with you!" I said scornfully. "What, after all, is wrong about being well read and educated? I don't scorn to admit it! Why, Mrs. Wollstonecraft said in her book—"

"Nothing wrong with it at all!" he said. "But it doesn't mean it can't get you in trouble. Discreet! That's the word to remember! *Especially* if you have read Mrs. Wollstonecraft. Why, the woman's a radical! Not saying that she doesn't make some good points." He paused thoughtfully here, then shook his head. "But she's put up any number of people's backs. You don't want to pass yourself off to be more than you are—or more than some people think you are. Wrong way to make a point."

I felt somewhat uncomfortable at that but said: "Well, I'll agree with part of what you said, but what should it matter if you show yourself to be better than what some people think you are?"

Lord Ashcombe looked uncomfortable. "Nothing again, if you are discreet about it. It's vulgar, don't you know, to trumpet your accomplishments all around town. I've said it can get you in trouble, and it can, I know!"

"From experience, no doubt!" I said.

"Yes, dash it!" he exclaimed, goaded. He sighed and looked at me. "I suppose it helps to have a few examples, doesn't it? It's really too bad you only have your mother and not a father as well— not," he said hastily, "that your mama has not done a good job of it." Lord Ashcombe paused. "You see, I remember everything I read," he said simply.

I looked at him blankly. "Well, so do most people, I would think."

He shook his head. "No, what I mean is, I only

have to read a thing once, and after I am done, I only have to think of the book and it's as if the thing were sitting there right before my eyes. It's all imprinted in here." He tapped his head.

I sat back in my chair, sniffed the posy he had given me, and looked at him warily. Either, I thought, he was making fun of me or he had something loose in the cockloft. He saw my skeptical look and became affronted.

"Well, I see you don't believe me." He looked around the sitting room and spotted a newspaper. "Here, give me that. Now, pick out any article you want, I'll read it, then repeat everything in it word for word." He slapped it down on my lap.

I leafed through it, chose an article, and gave the paper back to him, pointing at it.

He wrinkled his nose. "You *would* give me some boring piece about a charity ball." He scanned it for a minute and gave it back to me.

"That's all you are going to read of it?" I said, surprised. "You can't have finished it!"

"I have," he said shortly, closed his eyes, and recited: "'The well-known philanthropist Lady Rotheringham gave one of the best charity balls of the season: lavish in entertainment, refreshment, and the presence of the beau monde, this function was a success of the highest order. . . .'"

I listened with my mouth open as he repeated, word for word, the entire article. As he came near the end, he paused and said: "Surely you don't want me to continue this stuff, do you?"

"Yes, I mean, no, oh, please go on!" I said, awed. That someone could memorize the printed page at a glance! I stared at him in wonder as he finished.

"Well, you don't have to stare at me as if I were a dancing bear!" he said irritably.

"But how wonderful!" I exclaimed. "You probably did not have to study at all at Oxford, did you?"

"Not much," he said glumly. "That was rather a problem, really."

"How so?"

"How would you feel if someone you knew never had to study and got the highest honors in the class?"

"Amazed, I suppose, and somewhat envious."

"Replace 'amazed' with 'suspicious' and you have the picture. I had to demonstrate my 'talent' over and over again to my professors just to convince them I hadn't been cheating. It's hard not to come to feel like a sort of freak," he said morosely. "I once saw a mathematical pig at St. Bartholomew's Fair, tapping out its answers to two plus two, and I thought, There but for the Grace of God go I."

I had to smile at this, for Lord Ashcombe's looks were the farthest thing imaginable from those of a pig. "But after you convinced your professors, where was the problem?" I asked.

"Wasn't discreet about my ability, you see. It's what I've been trying to tell you." Lord Ashcombe went on to tell me that many of his fellow students knew of his ability, and while some were envious, most relied on him for help in their studies. It came to pass, however, that he came to cuffs with a strict and rather unpopular professor; a competent and learned man, he was like most, human and prone to mistakes. He delivered his lectures in a dry and humorless manner, and this always caused his students to be restless; Lord Ashcombe only fanned the flames by correcting him whenever he made mistakes, large or small.

For all his dry and unemotional delivery, however, the man had his limits; one day, the professor had grossly misquoted Marcus Aurelius, and Lord Ashcombe eagerly, tactlessly, caught him up and quoted the passage correctly. The professor fell silent. He sarcastically asked if his lordship wished to teach the class instead. Abashed, he murmured a negative but insisted *his* quote was right.

The professor pinned him with a steely eye and said that unless Lord Ashcombe would like to lecture in his place, he suggested that he keep his ideas to himself. There was a hiss in the back of the room, and a ball of rumpled paper bounced off the professor's balding pate. Soon the room was hailing balls of paper, and the professor, unable to control his students, fled.

Lord Ashcombe was soon summoned by the dean. While the dean was kindly, he sentenced him to a short suspension from the college. "We can't have a disruptive classroom, my boy," he said. "I realize the man is not the most popular teacher we have on this campus, but I think you knew this, and you must have seen that your undermining of his lectures was not going to make him any more popular." He sighed. "The man is not unreasonable, you know. Could you not have been a bit more tactful? You could have talked with him after classes and discussed his lecture then; far less embarrassing for the professor and quite a bit less disruptive in the classroom. Well, for now, the man can't stand the sight of you, and I think it best you leave until he can."

"So you see," said Lord Ashcombe, "I had to leave for a while just until things cooled down a bit."

"But that was unjust!" I cried. "Why, if you were in the right about the passage, your professor should have owned up to it—you shouldn't have been punished for it!"

He smiled and shook his head. "You still don't understand. Wasn't a matter of who was mistaken and who was not. The dean was in the right of it. I knew as well as anyone else that the professor was not popular, that the students in the class were restless. Knew my remarks about the lectures in front of all and sundry were a thorn in the man's side. Knew it very well. I was just so puffed up about how brainy I was that I didn't care if I interrupted the man or how he felt or even if I disrupted the classroom—which I knew could happen. Conceited. I *needed* a set-down. Good thing I got it *then*; won't have to suffer the cut direct by anyone now I know better. That's what being on the town is about, part of it, anyway. Knowing how to do the pretty, and being seen to your best advantage."

I reflected on this and had to concede to him. It *was* important to know how to behave, if only to avoid hurting people's feelings. For all that I had not grown up with a father, Mama *had* raised me with the Golden Rule, after all. I ruefully admitted to myself that it was something perhaps I needed help in; how many times had I snapped at poor Mama for no reason except bad temper? I sighed. "I see what you mean. But I don't see how it will do me any good. I don't see anyone except for Mama and, of course, you."

Lord Ashcombe shrugged. "I suppose you'll get into the way of things in your come-out."

"Yes! Thrust in the midst of activity and muddling everything dreadfully because I do not know how to go on. I don't know if I could bear it if I embarrassed poor Mama."

His lordship pondered this at length while I absently nibbled on a biscuit, imagining all the terrible scrapes I would fall into just because I knew nothing about life in the ton. "Practice!" he said suddenly.

I was startled out of my reverie of horrors, and the biscuit fell from my hand, breaking in crumbly pieces in my lap. "Now look at what you've done!" I exclaimed.

Caught up in his thoughts, he ignored me. "Practice!" he repeated. "That's what you need. Practice now, and when the time comes, you'll go on as smooth as cream! I'll help." He beamed, pleased at himself.

My heart hammered in excitement, but I said cautiously, "How can you do that?"

"Take you out and about, show you the sights, let you know what's what. That's how!"

I shook my head. "If you think that is the way to make Mama believe we have not a *tendre* for each other, you are mightily mistaken, my lord!"

This silenced him for a while as he thought his idea over. He brightened. "Got it! I have a sister. Actually, I have four sisters." His pleased expression wilted somewhat, then revived. "All but the last ages older than I am. Samantha's the one I'm thinking of, just as old as you are, not quite out of the schoolroom yet; bound to like an outing or two. Propose an outing, have m'mater issue an invitation to you, and there we are!"

I still felt dubious. "I still think Mama will see you as being most particular in your attentions."

He threw up his hands in disgust. "*Do* you want to do this or *don't* you? I don't see that it matters what your mother thinks at this point, especially since she already thinks we're as close as promised to each other and nothing will convince her to the contrary!"

I agreed with a sigh that this was true. "But what will your mother think?"

"Nothing at all," he replied promptly. "Probably grateful to get Samantha off her hands for a while. You'll like her, I know. Samantha, I mean. I do myself."

I could see no real flaws in his plan. I grew excited again to think I would no longer be tied only to reading and being walked by a maid to and from shops. Certainly his idea was as good as—perhaps better than—any I had had! I looked admiringly at Lord Ashcombe. "Oh, it's a wonderful plan! And so kind of you to help me in this way! I know I will enjoy myself excessively!"

He blushed and disclaimed, "Not at all, not at all. Just returning a favor. After all, if it hadn't been for you, I might have found myself leg-shackled to your mother! Not that it's not what a man would want, but I'm rather a bit young for that sort of thing, you know! Still want to kick up a few larks before I settle down, after all!"

Impulsively I clasped his hand, briefly raised it to my cheek, and lifted my eyes to his. "Oh, but you are too modest, I know! How kind you are! I am so grateful! I know I shall like meeting your sister!"

He opened his mouth and closed it, staring down at me for a long moment before saying, "Yes, well, er, yes. N-nothing, really, trifling service, no need to make anything of it." He seemed to shake himself a bit. "It'll be a treat for my sister, too; good to know more people her own age, eh?" He let out a puff of breath and straightened his waistcoat with a brisk air. "Well, that's that, then! I shall see if I can set something up for next week, if that is all right with you?" I nodded.

A thought seemed to strike him. "Good God, Samantha will probably be in transports over this—hasn't been out and about for months! I'll have to keep my distance when I tell her, or she'll be casting herself at my waistcoat and rumpling my cravat no end! Never knew such a one for hugging and petting her relations. A man's not a curst spaniel, you know!"

He shook his head. "Sisters!" he uttered disgustedly.

4

Mother handed me the invitation from Samantha with raised brows that said "I told you so" as clearly as if she had spoken. I ignored this. I, at least, knew the true state of affairs, if Mama did not. That would suffice until such time as Lord Ashcombe became seriously attached to someone else; then she would know she had been mistaken in the direction of his affections. Meanwhile, I would enjoy his company and that of his sister in our outings, all with Mama's approval.

I felt a moment of guilt, wondering if I were taking selfish advantage of Mama's stubborn hopes for me, but reflected that even if she did believe that Lord Ashcombe and I were only friends, she could hardly object to—indeed, she might even encourage—my making friends with respectable people of my own age.

His lordship was right. I did like Samantha. As we quickly came to know each other, we turned "Miss Canning" and "Miss Ashcombe" into Georgia and Samantha. With Lord Ashcombe becoming very much like a brother to me, I came to call him Lucas as Samantha did. She was very like her brother in coloring: very wavy black hair, with clear translucent skin that became stained a light cherry about her cheeks when she became animated. Her eyes were not so blue as Lord Ashcombe's—they were more of a bluish green, almost aqua color—but her lashes were as enviably long. She was slim and neat as a pin, but not as tall as I had expected she would be after seeing her brother. Indeed, I had thought I was short, but I must have topped her by almost four inches. She was a bit shy and quiet at first, but when I revealed to her my scholastic ambitions, she grew more lively and disclosed that she, too, had ambitions: she wished to be a Writer of Novels.

Lord Ashcombe listened to these revelations with what was clearly a superior air and too obvious tolerance as he quite expertly tooled our carriage down Rotten Row. Samantha caught his eye and said: "And I don't want to hear anything from *you* about if it is worth doing or not, because I am determined to Write. I was *born* to do so! I am sure of it!" She lifted her little chin, looked at me, and nodded her head with assurance. I nodded back. I had to admire someone with serious ambitions and the determination to carry them out.

Lucas shook his head. "If I ever saw two chits less suited toward your 'ambitions,' I don't remember 'em! Why, I haven't seen you lift a pen, Sam, since Miss Jamieson left to visit her mother! As for writing letters, who was it that was two weeks late writing thank-you notes after Christmas, may I ask?"

Samantha retorted, "Well, I did finally write them, and they were good ones, too! Better than yours, at any rate! And longer! Besides, an Author must be Inspired! One just does not write any insipid thing down on paper. As for writing since Miss Jamieson left, why, you don't think I would show my writing to just anyone, do you?" She sniffed haughtily and sat back against the cushions on her seat, arms tucked in her muffler.

It seemed to me that she was in the right of it, but I turned to Lord Ashcombe and asked: "And what is it about me that isn't suited toward teaching and scholarship?"

He pondered this a moment. "Don't doubt that you're intelligent enough, you know your geography and books and all that. Thing is, you're too pretty."

I gasped and blushed. "Well, of all the whiskers! You're quite wrong about that, I know! I have grown up with Mama, you might remember, and I know what pretty is! Now, tell me the true reason you think I would not be suited to being a governess. No flim-flamming about, if you please!"

"Not flim-flamming at all! Not saying you're as beautiful as your mama—different coloring, for one thing—but you have a look of her, enough to make a man sit up and take notice. Not trying to put you to the blush," he said, looking at my flushed face. "Ask Samantha! Got a 'Writer's eye.' She would know," he ended with some irony.

I turned to Samantha questioningly. She nodded. "Oh, yes, Georgia, Lucas is right! I don't know what your mama looks like, but you are prettier than most young ladies I have seen, and I have seen many, both at home and out the window, for you must know my window looks out on the square and I can see ever so many people! It is very useful for me as a writer; I note down in my journal everything about the people I see just in case I might use it sometime in a story."

I felt suddenly shy, for I had never seriously considered myself pretty; Mama was always the standard I went by, and I had not thought that one could not look like her but be thought handsome on one's own. "Th-thank you!" I murmured, eyes downcast. "I feel you must be mistaken, but it is very kind in you to compliment me so." My mind turned inexorably, however, back to Lucas's comment about being too pretty for teaching. "Even so," I said briskly, raising a firm eye to his, "what do one's looks have to do with teaching? If one is learned and a competent teacher, that should be qualification enough, I should think!"

"Qualifications!" snorted Lucas. "That's all well and good, but pretty governesses ain't hired. Think about it. What did your governesses or schoolmistresses look like?"

I did think about it and was silent, for though

there were many schoolmistresses I liked, none of them could be said to be above passably good-looking.

"You see? Passable, some of 'em, but others are out-and-out antidotes!"

Samantha looked, puzzled, at her brother. "But why is that so? Georgia is right; the way one looks shouldn't have bearing on whether one is hired or not—it should be because one is a competent teacher. In fact, you didn't really answer her question, you know! You just said pretty governesses simply aren't hired. That is not an answer!"

Lucas shifted uncomfortably on his seat, caught sight of a familiar face, and hailed the passerby. It was a while before all the introductions were done and his acquaintance was on his way, but Samantha was persistent. "Now that you've tried to make me forget the subject, but failed, do let us get back to it." She somehow managed to insert a hint of steel into her softly smiling voice. I laughed.

"Wasn't trying to make you forget anything—not that it wouldn't have been a good thing! Can't cut an acquaintance, after all! Bad ton!" he protested indignantly.

"Lucas!"

"Oh, dash it all!" He sighed. "Pretty governesses ain't hired because it'd cause trouble. Especially if there are male members of the family around."

Samantha's brow furrowed. "But I don't see—"

"I do," I said. Lucas was staring out above the horses' ears, apparently concentrating on squeezing between a phaeton and a wagon, but his cheeks had grown a bit pink. "You're saying that a man of the family might fall in love—or worse—with the governess if she were pretty. And it isn't proper that such a thing should happen." I had read of this in some of the novels Mama borrowed from the circulating library—but it had come out all right in the end. Perhaps it was different in real life.

"Well, if that isn't the most unjust thing I have ever heard!" Samantha exclaimed.

Her brother shrugged his shoulders. "Not saying it isn't, but think: If you were hiring someone and thought her presence might cause some trouble, and things would be nice and calm if you simply did not hire her, wouldn't you take that road? Simple as can be. Wouldn't have to watch things every minute, rely on a plain woman's looks to keep the air cool, teach your children at the same time." Samantha looked troubled, but again, I had to admit he was right.

"It still isn't just!" cried Samantha, not wanting to give up.

"Wish there were something I could do about it, but it can't be helped." Lucas snapped the whip just above the horses' ears, and we slid past the wagon. "Just the way things are."

"Perhaps I could become a schoolmistress, if not a governess," I pursued hopefully. "I wouldn't encounter many men in a young ladies' academy like Miss Angstead's, I am sure."

"If," replied Lucas dampingly, "there isn't a painting master or one of those dancing masters about. Might fall head over heels for you, and then what will you do? Can't have that sort of thing happening in a school, I imagine."

I thought of the dancing master at Miss Angstead's and doubted that this would ever occur. Signore Trapelli, contrary to my preferred image of Italians, was a dour, sallow, spindle-shanked little man; he could dance elegantly to the most liveliest music and never change his basset-hound countenance to anything more cheerful than a brief grimace of teeth. I could not imagine Signore Trapelli falling head over heels for anyone. I shrugged and cast a skeptical glance at Lucas. Catching it, he said: "That is, if there's a position available for you at all. Seems like there's any number of females looking for a position like that all the time."

That sent me to point non plus as none of his other arguments did. I well knew the number of young women who applied at Miss Angstead's Seminary for Young Ladies and how many were turned away, for it was seldom that a position became vacant, and when it did, it was not for long. I had always assumed that I would take a position as a governess or schoolmistress when I came of age, for I did not want to be a burden to Mama. I had not considered other options, for my love of scholarship was really the one thing that occupied my mind and my time. I felt at quite a loss.

Samantha saw my crestfallen face and tried to help. "Well, how about millinery?" she said tentatively.

"I don't know anything about making hats," I

said, "unless I could paint them. I suppose I could design some dresses, but I can hardly sew a straight seam, much less know how one could make a living designing dresses."

We rode in silence for a while, when suddenly Lucas spoke up. "Dash it all, don't see why we have to make a big thing of it! Thing is, don't see why you think you have to have an occupation."

"Not have an occupation! Why, why, of course I do! I can not be a burden on Mama once I come of age! She has had enough to bear!"

Lord Ashcombe clicked his tongue in impatience. "Wouldn't *be* a burden on your mama if you *married*!"

"Lucas is right!" exclaimed Samantha. "How silly of me not to think of it! I suppose you were so bent on being a governess that I was led to think that was your only fate! Then, too, I have never thought of my ambition as being exclusive of marriage, while you, it seems, have been thinking so of your own. Stupid of me, really; I should have *thought* . . . ! I have never known a governess who was also married!"

"B-but I have not thought of marriage," I stammered.

Two pairs of blue eyes stared at me incredulously.

"Well, of all the—!"

"How can you not think—" blurted brother and sister at the same time.

They looked at each other humorously for a moment, then Samantha nodded for Lucas to go ahead. "Well, of all the nonsense I have ever heard, that one beats everything! Not thought of marriage! My word!"

I opened my mouth to speak, but Samantha interrupted, glaring at her brother. "You gudgeon! That's the last time I let you speak first! Merciful heavens! If your berating her isn't the best way to make marriage repulsive to her, I do not know what is!" She cast a scornful look at Lucas.

"Respect for your elders, my girl, that's what you don't know!" he retorted with a superior air.

"Respect for my—! Bah!" she uttered in accents of extreme disgust.

Silence reigned for a few moments, but I could not hold back my laughter. At my initial giggle, two pairs of offended eyes turned toward me, but then they lightened, and Samantha joined in the laughter, while Lucas relaxed and smiled.

"That was beastly of us, having a row in front of you," Samantha apologized. "But Lucas *will* speak before he thinks!" She glanced laughingly at Lucas, who maintained an expression of long-suffering martyrdom—not for long, however, for his eyes twinkled suddenly, and he nudged his sister with his elbow.

"Obnoxious chit!" he said affectionately. "I hope your husband takes you firmly in hand; he'd be living under the sign of the cat's foot, else!"

"That is not, dear Georgia, what husbands are for," said Samantha, turning to me.

"As if you knew!" muttered Lucas.

His sister ignored him. "Now I am curious. Why haven't you thought of marriage? I have ambitions, too, but that hasn't deterred *me* from thinking of it."

I pondered this. "I do not know," I said slowly. "I have just been absorbed with my studies as far as I can remember, and I suppose I did not think there was much else. Then, too, Mama has remained unmarried so long that the idea of having a man about the house is not one that comes naturally to me." I shook my head again and shrugged.

Samantha looked at me with kind pity. I felt heat creeping up to my cheeks; I had never thought that I might be an object of pity, and the idea did not sit well with me. But I did feel glad that she was friend enough to care. She took my hand in hers and pressed it. "Well, it is about time you did think of it. Certainly your admirers will think of it when they see you."

Lucas nodded in agreement. "That's what I've been telling you," he said briskly. "Need to get out and about, acquire some Town bronze, let yourself be seen. There's any number of possibilities out in the world."

"Yes!" exclaimed Samantha. "Mama has been thinking of giving a small party for me, just to let me get used to such a setting. I will ask that you be invited. Then you will be able to get as much practice as I. Everyone is to dress as if we are already presented, too! It will be ever so much fun!"

"Good girl!" approved her brother. "Thought you might have something aside from sawdust in that brainbox of yours, but I wasn't sure." Samantha wrinkled her nose at him.

I laughed. "I must thank you! I do hope Mama will allow me to go! I am sure it will be most enjoyable."

"Don't think why she'd object. Let you come along for a carriage ride, didn't she?" Lucas said.

"But a party—!"

"All the more reason to let you go," he replied cynically. His sister glanced quizzically at him. He looked embarrassed but said: "Her mother wants to throw us together, you see. Thinks to, ah, encourage, ah, interests."

I could see a speculative gleam growing in her eye, and apparently Lucas saw this, too, for he expostulated: "Now, don't you be getting any ideas! Thing is, too young! Both of us! Besides, you heard her! Hadn't thought of marriage! Not a thing to get used to in a twinkling, either—needs time!" He ran a finger between cravat and neck, eyeing his sister warily.

She did not look at him and seemed to be staring at a passing tobacco shop window. "Hmm," she murmured. She turned to me. "Well, at any rate, Georgia, you will certainly have the opportunity to meet people. Who knows, perhaps a future swain will be there who will eventually sweep you off your feet and carry you off!"

Lucas snorted, but I ignored him. "That may be the problem," I said thoughtfully. I replied to their questioning looks: "If I were to be 'carried off,' as you say, what will become of Mama?" Samantha looked blank. "She will be all alone, for she has no husband to depend on. There is only myself. And I mean to be a prop to her as long as she lacks that support."

Lucas remarked, "But didn't you say Sir Jeremy had asked her to wife?"

"Yes," I replied, "but I also said she refused him."

Samantha's eyes widened, and I proceeded to explain the situation to her and some of Mama's reasons for refusing Sir Jeremy. Not all of them, of course.

"Oh, how romantic! And how noble of your mother!" exclaimed Samantha.

I nodded glumly. "And how impractical," I said. "It is clear to anyone looking at them that they are top over tails in love. Sir Jeremy knows that my grandfather was a merchant. If he does not mind, why should Mama?"

Lucas shrugged. "Female scruples," he said.

"Well, I am a female, but I don't have such scruples!" I pointed out.

Samantha raised her hands in a gesture of peace. "Now, Georgia, I do see you are right, for I would not have such scruples, either. But Lucas is right, too; the Older Generation, you know," she said wisely, "do not quite have the same notions as we do." I reflected that this was true. There were any number of things Mama had said to me that did not make practical sense but were "what ladies do."

"I wish there were something I could do to make her change her mind!" I said, frustrated. "I had had all sorts of plans when I first came home, and now they are all to pieces and I *cannot* think of any others! If I could think of some way to have them marry, I could go governessing in peace." I caught Lord Ashcombe's skeptical eye and amended tartly, "Or marry."

"Perhaps"—Samantha sighed hopefully—"we can think of something by and by." She exchanged a look with her brother that I could not read. Smiling kindly at me, she took my hand again. "Meanwhile, we shall have fun, shall we not? I am looking forward to my party, and to having you there, too! How nice it is to become friends!" she exclaimed.

My spirits could not help but lighten at her words, and I returned her press of hands and smiled at her and then at Lucas. Lucas looked seriously back at me for a moment, then grinned. When I glanced back at his sister, I thought I saw a little smile on her lips—but it was quickly gone.

It was not long after this that Mama gave me another note, this time with a smile more smug than the last. We were sitting in the parlour with a small repast and, as was growing more usual lately, with Sir Jeremy. "From Lady Ashcombe, I see. Not another carriage ride, I presume?" Mama's smile grew even more smug—if that were possible.

I rolled my eyes heavenward. "Oh, Mama, really! It was just a simple carriage ride with Lord Ashcombe and his sister, Samantha! We are growing to be good friends, I think. She is quite amiable. *That* was what the ride was all about; his lordship thought it might be a good thing if we were to become friends, primarily because poor Samantha was getting bored in London by herself. Her governess, Miss Jamieson, is away visiting her sick mother, so she doesn't have much to occupy herself."

Mama nodded wisely. "Ah, primarily for you to become friends with his sister. And secondarily?" she teased.

I blushed and sighed in exasperation. "Mother! Please!" I threw an agonized glance at Sir Jeremy, who only smiled benignly. Mama laughed. I knew there was no arguing with her.

I turned over the gilt-edged note and broke the seal. It was the invitation to Samantha's party, as she had promised. I smiled. "Mama, look! Samantha has invited me to her party, just as she said she would. Do say I can go! It is to be an informal sort of thing, just to become comfortable around guests and learn how to go on."

Mama threw a triumphant look at Sir Jeremy, who simply lifted his brows. Her glance seemed to contain a challenge, and I was sure it had to do with my receiving an invitation to Samantha's party. I wondered if Sir Jeremy had approached Mama from the point of being a father to me; it seemed likely, if Mama's challenging glance was any indication. I knew she took pride in the fact that she had raised me by herself, despite the difficulties in being a woman alone. I looked again at Sir Jeremy and was startled to see his eye slowly wink. An idea flashed suddenly in my mind.

"Of course you can go!" cried Mama. "I would not have you miss it for the world! We shall have to make you a new dress, of course. Now let us see . . ." She drifted off, thinking of colors, patterns, and fabrics.

I sighed soulfully. "Oh, Mama, I am so glad you

approve! Lord Ashcombe will be there as well, you know. Do you not think he is *so* very handsome?"

Mama swung around to stare at me, startled out of her sartorial dreams by my sudden switch of direction. I dropped my gaze shyly, but not before I caught Sir Jeremy's quizzical look from beneath my lashes. "Why, why, yes, I believe he is. Do you like him, then, Georgia?" Her voice sounded breathless, tentative.

"Oh, Mama!" I fluttered, and shyly turned my face away from her. As I turned, I briefly glanced at Sir Jeremy's face and saw that it had become very, very still; but there was that bright, mischievous look in his eyes, and his shoulders shook oh, so very slightly. I felt like laughing, too, and my efforts not to made me flush brightly—and very opportunely. "So kind!" I continued in a breathless voice. "So fine in his sensibilities! So quick in understanding!"

"Oh, my dear! My dear, dear, girl!" exclaimed Mama. "It is more than I had hoped for! Has he said—? Has he indicated—?" She had flown out of her chair to embrace me in a flurry of perfume and silk.

"Oh, please, Mama!" I glanced again at Sir Jeremy. Mama caught this and waved a hand at him.

"Perhaps you have another engagement, Jeremy?" she said. This was not what I wanted. I shot a look of entreaty at him.

"None that I can think of," Sir Jeremy said obligingly.

Mama pursed her lips, trying to think of a way

to dismiss him politely, but I said: "It is quite all right if Sir Jeremy stays, Mama. Truly. Why he is—*almost*—like a father to me. I do not mind if we confide in him." I smiled sweetly at him. His lips twitched upward briefly, but he managed to keep the rest of his face composed.

"I am honored," he said gravely.

Mama looked a bit confused. "But if you do not mind Sir Jeremy's presence, why did you hesitate, love?"

I gave her a reproachful look. "Such a delicate subject," I murmured. "I hesitate to say what Lord Ashcombe's actions might—might *entail*." I subsided in maidenly modesty.

Mama looked from me to Sir Jeremy and back again. An expression of dawning horror came over her face. "Oh, my dear girl! Never say that Lord Ashcombe—that he has tried to, to take advantage of you! Was *that* why you wished Sir Jeremy to stay?"

I jerked and sat up straight on my chair. That Sir Jeremy met my indignant eyes with a wide grin over Mama's head and *definitely* shaking shoulders did nothing to abate my affronted sensibilities. "Of course not!" I exclaimed scornfully. Her face grew puzzled at my tone of voice, but I recovered and said with what I hoped was a lovelorn sigh, "He is so gentlemanly, Mama! And he introduced me to his *sister*! How could you think—! He could not be so common, Mama!"

She sighed with relief and said hastily: "No, no, my dear! I see I was sadly mistaken. Of course he would not compromise you! He is an exceptional young man, I know. But"—she looked at me tentatively—"have you any, ah, indications where his affections may, ah, lie?"

"I believe I will be introduced to Lady Ashcombe, his mother," I said, knowing that Samantha would do so at the party. If Mama wished to think that Lucas was going to do so, I would not disabuse her of this idea.

She smiled tremulously at me and dabbed at a tear with her hand. I gave her a handkerchief I had in my pocket. "Oh, Georgia, my dear daughter! I am so happy! How wonderfu—"

"Alas!" I sighed, interrupting her. "It is all for naught, however!" I looked sadly at the ceiling, clasping my hands in my lap. From the corner of my eyes, I saw Sir Jeremy's eyebrows quirk up. He leaned back on his chair with a little smile and crossed his legs: the better to enjoy the show, I thought. I felt slightly put out.

"Why, whatever can you mean?" said Mama, startled.

"Whatever his intentions, or anyone else's, dear Mama, I cannot marry! Surely you must see that!" I clasped her hands in mine and looked at her lovingly. Mama looked thoroughly bewildered.

"Why, Mama, how can you think I would desert you, alone in the world, when you have devoted your love and constant energies to my welfare? Did you think you brought me up to be a selfish, thoughtless daughter? Why do you think I have studied long and hard at Miss Angstead's school? I mean to be a support and prop to you, Mama!" I said this with all the sincerity I could muster—

which was considerable, for indeed, I had always thought of this as the natural way I would live my life.

"B-but, my dear, you can't—you cannot think I wanted you to be an *old maid*!"

I spread my hands and shrugged my shoulders. "What does it matter to me if I remain a spinster? Nothing. The thought of a child abandoning her parent in loneliness while enjoying the fruits of marriage is abhorrent to me, I assure you, Mama. I know I have been impertinent and not always the ideal daughter to you," I said humbly, "but never let it be said I have dishonored my mother or my father!"

Mama stared at me aghast. She tottered backward from me, groping for a chair, and was tenderly escorted by Sir Jeremy to a settee. He sat next to her and patted her hands. "Now, now, Celia, is this so surprising?" he murmured. "You have told me—often and often—what a good and wonderful daughter Georgia is, and so she is showing herself to be! Her sentiments do her—and you—credit. Why should she not stay at your side, caring for you?"

She turned, looking blindly at him. "But, Jeremy, she is so lovely, and so young! Not marry! Why, it would be a cruel waste, she would never know—"

"What you and I would have had?" cut in Sir Jeremy, looking at her with warm tenderness in his eyes. Mama became still and gazed at him with an arrested expression.

She tore her eyes away. "Y— No! That is not what I mean!" She turned to me. "Listen, darling.

Do you not think it would be a wonderful thing to
have a family, and children?"

I pretended to ponder this. "I don't know," I
said. "We do well enough, you and I, don't we? And
with Sir Jeremy visiting, of course, we are almost a
family, I imagine." I smiled at him in a friendly
manner. "Besides, if I were to have children, there
would be less time for me to care for you, Mama!"

"Perhaps . . . perhaps you don't really care for
Lord Ashcombe?" asked Mama, grasping at
straws.

I made my chin tremble, my eyes downcast,
and I hugged my arms as if protecting myself from
the sorrows of the world. "I . . . will get over it,
Mama. Truly. And think: If I were to succumb to
my . . . my affections for him, how could I live with
the fact that you would have no one to comfort
and succor you in times of need?"

"Oh, Georgia, you needn't think of me! I have
friends!"

I looked at her kindly, but steadily, in the eye.
"But that is not the same as family," I said. "And I
am the only family you have." I went over to
where she was sitting with Sir Jeremy and patted
her hand. "I can manage, Mama," I said with a
tremulous sigh. "Lord Ashcombe will understand
that his attentions cannot deter me from what I
know is my true course in life. Perhaps . . . perhaps
we can remain friends. It is what I hope."

Mama, frozen in Sir Jeremy's protecting arms,
stared at me as if I were a cockatrice. I smiled
lovingly, if sadly, at both of them before I rose to
leave the room. I opened the door and turned

once more to them, saying: "I know where my duty lies, dear Mama; you cannot dissuade me, for I know how unselfishly you will try to convince me otherwise." I stepped out of the sitting room, closing the door. I leaned against the doorjamb, waiting.

A sudden wail erupted from the room I had just left. "Oh, Jeremy, Jeremy! This was not what I wanted at all! What have I done?"

I let loose a sigh of relief, grinning, then curt-sied to a cheering—and imaginary—audience. Ah, success!

5

Mama watched me warily for two weeks. I think the change in my demeanor had made her suspicious. While I had always been attentive to her, on the day she handed me the invitation to Samantha's party, my manner was certainly touched with a martyrlike air and my concern for her was almost cloying. I had reverted back to my own cheerful ways almost immediately, however, for I was sure it would serve no purpose for me to remain a Tragedy Jill. First, such a drastic change from my own nature would certainly be unconvincing, and second, it was a tiresome act to keep up.

I found it a wise decision. My apparent unchanged personality, accented by a few kindly services for Mama and an occasional sad and abstracted mien, apparently convinced her as nothing else would have that I was firm in my conviction that my destiny was to become a lovelorn but devoted spinster, supporting my beloved mother in her declining years.

That I had found two friends in the interim between plans did nothing to dissipate my glee. After years in school with the only result being a well-educated mind and no friends at all, I now had a well-educated mind and friends who could accept that in me. If I wished, I could discuss the classics and even Mrs. Wollstonecraft's works when I was with Lucas. His own interests were more practical in matter, however; his father had died of an apoplexy when Lucas was nineteen, leaving him with three different properties to manage. Of course, Lucas's solicitors and agents did the daily supervision, and Lucas need not have involved himself at all. But he took an interest in farming and in the mills on his properties and actively sought to do as much as he could with them.

"Thing is," he said one day while he, Samantha, and I set out on an al fresco luncheon, "it's deuced difficult to get what improvements I want done in both the mills and the estates—not quite of age, you see."

"But they are *your* estates, after all!" I said. "Surely that counts for something."

"Of course it does." Lucas shrugged. "But I must go through my trustees first, and it's dashed difficult reasoning with them."

"They are terribly old-fashioned," chimed in

Samantha. "They act as if younger heads cannot have more than two thoughts in them to rub together!"

"Hidebound!" said Lucas. "Can't think beyond two years in the future. Take my millhands, for instance. I want to pay them a touch more than they're earning now, enough to reduce their hours a bit. I *have* managed to take the children out of there, thank God, but my trustees are balking at my setting up schools and nurseries for them."

Samantha beamed at him. "Why, Lucas, I did not know you were going to set up schools for the children!"

"How truly kind you are!" I exclaimed, and gazed at him in admiration.

"Not kind at all!" protested Lucas. He looked embarrassed, and his ears took on a pink color. "I mean to say, it's only practical!" He nodded his head toward the horses he was driving. "Think! No good horseman drives his horses at a spanking pace for sixteen hours at a time—it'd ruin 'em. Stands to reason a man's not as strong as a horse. You ruin a man, and then you have to start all over training another—waste of time, because you know a new man won't work as well as one who has done it before. Shorten the hours, keep 'em in good health, pay 'em a bit more to make up for it, and you've got good workers that last a long time. Not only that, but the good workers will stay with you because Lord only knows they wouldn't get better work elsewhere."

"But what of the schools? How is that going to make for better millhands?" asked Samantha.

Lucas looked more embarrassed and shifted uncomfortably on his seat. "Haven't thought up a good argument for that yet. Heard of the idea from a mill owner, Robert Owens, up in Lancashire. Sounded like a good one."

I smiled to myself. So much for being "only practical"! I felt a warmth grow in me: how kind and modest he was! Few mill owners would think twice about the welfare of their workers. *I* knew firsthand of Lucas's kindness—had he not been so to me? It did not surprise me that it extended to his dependents as well.

It is remarkable how things all fall together when one has a Plan. Samantha and I discussed my abilities at length and had now found another occupation for me besides that of schoolmistress. We had decided my talent for painting could be developed to the point of salability. It would be difficult, said Samantha, for she had heard of only one woman, Angelica Kauffmann, making a living at it, but this challenge gave me greater fuel for practice.

I reserved a few hours of each day for practicing my drawing, sketching, and painting, and Mama once ventured into the schoolroom, curious. She stood behind me for a while, watching as I charcoal-sketched a bowl of fruit on a table. I was not aware of her presence for a while, for I was absorbed in the shapes and shadows cast by the apples and grapes in the earthenware bowl, and my eyes turned from the arrangement only to follow the lines I made with the charcoal stick on paper or my fingers when I smoothed a black line into grey roundedness.

"That is well done," came Mama's voice behind me.

Startled, I turned, then smiled at her. "Thank you, Mama. I felt it was time I practiced what I learned at Miss Angstead's. Miss Tarnaby, the drawing mistress, once told me I had a talent for it. I think it a pity should I lose the ability through lack of practice, do not you?"

"Indeed! Quite a waste! Tell me, what subject do you plan to try next?"

I thought about this for a minute, then brightened. "Lord Ashcombe and Samantha have invited me to an al fresco luncheon in the country if the weather complies. I suppose I could try a landscape then."

Mama glowed. "Why, how wonderful! How amiable of his lordship and his sister to invite you! I know you will have a very enjoyable time with him—them."

I sighed wistfully and my smile faded as I said: "Yes, Luc—ah, Lord Ashcombe is so very kind and—and handsome, is he not?" I turned back to my drawing. "I think I will have to get some oil paints for this drawing."

"Oil paints?" asked Mama, taken aback. "Do you not mean water colours? We could frame it and put it in the drawing room."

"Oh, no, Mama, definitely oils!" I said firmly. "Oils *sell,* you know. Water colours are only for one's own home or perhaps printed in books. If I am to sell miniatures or painted fans like Angelica Kauffmann, I will definitely have to practice more in oils."

"Sell?" Mama said faintly.

"Yes, I believe in having as many options as possible for a career," I said cheerfully. "If I cannot find a position as a governess or schoolmistress to support us in the future, perhaps I can fall back on my talent in painting. Indeed, I believe painting to be the superior choice. I can stay home with you and care for you then, instead of going away to earn money and leaving you all alone."

I turned and smiled at her as if expecting approval. She had closed her eyes as if in pain and was fumbling for the door. "Excuse me," she said weakly. "I think I forgot to tell Grimley about, about something. . . ."

She hurriedly quit the schoolroom, and I returned to my drawing with a smile and wider sweeps of the charcoal stick.

Samantha's party was looming fast, and I was both excited and anxious about it. Needless to say, I had had no experience with parties except Mama's at home, and I had been considered too young to attend those. I had watched them from the stairs while munching on tartlets and lemonade that Cook would furtively give me on these occasions, and I had observed some of the formalities of these gatherings. I felt I knew little and had more to learn. I was excited that at last I would be able to attend a party as a young lady already "out" would.

Mama brought a seamstress in to make me a dress for the event. We went through a number of Ackermann's fashion plates before we selected a round gown of pale blue muslin. My eyes had widened considerably when I surveyed the dresses displayed in these plates, which ranged from plain morning day dresses to sumptuous court gowns. Some, like the day dresses, were modestly cut with high necklines and ruffs; others such as ball gowns were so low cut as to make me think there had been an error in the printing of the drawings. I laughingly pointed out one of these to Mama, wondering aloud how these misprints could have got past the editors, but then she shook her head, saying they were not misprints at all.

I eyed Mama's fully developed bosom and my own not-quite-as-buxom one and said, "But, but Mama, unless they looked more like myself, I don't know how—how any lady could stay *in*!"

Mama broke out in her rich, trilling laugh. "It is something only women have figured out and are not telling the male members of the species. That mystery, I am sure, has gained the riveted attention of men since the décolletage was first discovered, and they seem *not* to have found the answer yet! Precisely why ladies continue to wear such dresses, my dear!"

The thought was daunting. I never had much cause to think of fashion in the past, for I was used to the schoolgirl's plain fare of neutrally colored, comfortably baggy round gowns that hid everything from neck to toe. When I came home, we bought more clothes for me, but these also were plain and modest, since I had outgrown my old gowns and had to have new ones in a hurry. But now I saw that these dresses à la mode exposed much more than I was used to, and I was not at all sure that I had anything worthy to expose—or wanted to. To be sure, I had seen Mama wear very fashionable clothes indeed. But she wore them naturally, unselfconsciously, and I knew I could never do so, for she had her beauty to support her and I did not. Even if I did have some measure of beauty, I knew I would feel, well, vulnerable somehow. Naked. I could feel my face growing warm at the thought. No, really, I could not wear such a dress.

I said: "So if a lady wishes to have a gentleman pay attention to her, she might wear one of these dresses?"

"That is one strategy, yes—especially if she has one such good feature and not any other attributes or talents which may attract."

"Well, I shall not need any such stratagems, thank goodness," I said firmly.

Mama smiled, saying: "No, indeed! You are quite pretty and lively enough so that you would not need to do so."

I blushed at this but said calmly, "Not at all, Mama! Indeed, I shall insist on having the neckline of my dress raised, as I have no wish to attract gentlemen at all! It will not do at all if I am to remain single and care for you, you see."

Mama froze slightly but seemed to recover; there even seemed to be a little gleam in her eye as she gazed at me for a short space of time. "Indeed!" she replied, her face serene.

I made sure, when the pattern came to be fitted about me, that Miss Barton knew to make the neckline high. She nodded and wrote this down in her little brown book and adjusted the pattern this way and that about me. Mama made no comment but merely smiled.

I grew a little worried. A fortnight after I had announced my intentions to be a prop to her, Mama no longer seemed to make such a fuss about it. I kept a watchful eye on her as I ran my little errands for her, but her reactions to my intentions for our future seemed to become less and less overt. Perhaps, I thought, she believed this turn of mine to be an errant whim that would pass with time. Well, we shall see who can wait the longest, I said to myself.

Meanwhile, Samantha called upon me, and we would discuss everything from the plots of stories she would write to my painting efforts to her party. We talked most about her party, as it was so near, and what we would wear. Samantha had chosen a white muslin dress with a rose-pink bodice and matching ribbons threaded through the tiny puffed sleeves. She showed me a picture of it from Ackermann's, only the plate showed the dress to have a yellow bodice.

"I simply cannot abide yellow—or orange, for that matter—so I nearly passed this design for another. But Mama pointed out that the bodice could just as well be made in another color, and so I agreed to it. I do wish, though, that I could see what it would look like in rose pink," she finished wistfully.

I nodded, then said suddenly: "I have an idea! I have some pastel chalks!"

Samantha looked bewildered at this apparent change of subject but waited.

"I will get some and paper, and I will draw what you would look like in that rose-pink dress!"

She clasped her hands together, starry-eyed. "Oh, could you? It would be wonderful if you did!"

"Of course!" I ran up to the schoolroom, fetched some paper, lead, and pastels, and brought them down again. I had Samantha stand near the light and put the fashion plate beside me. I sketched her basic features first, then, looking at the plate, imagined the dress on her and sketched it in. I brought the initial sketch to her for approval.

"Why, Georgia, it looks just like me! And as if I were really wearing the dress!" She wrinkled her brow for a moment as she looked at the plate. "The only difference, though, is that the neckline of the dress is lower cut in the plate than you have drawn it on me. Mama said it would look exactly like this for me except for the color." My eyes widened a bit, for the plate showed quite a décolletage. Samantha caught my surprised look and lifted an eyebrow. "Are you thinking that it is too low cut? I had thought so, too, but Mama says it is all the crack, I assure you!"

I nodded, reflecting that my dress with its neckline at the collarbone was probably going to look positively Quakerish. I mentally shrugged, however. It meant little to me if I was not precisely in mode, for I was not looking for a husband, after all.

I returned to my sketch, made the dress match the plate, and began to use the pastels. I used charcoal for Samantha's raven-black hair, and instead of drawing her hair in the schoolgirlish manner it was in, I had it pulled up in a knot with long ringlets falling forward toward her face. Tiny pink dots representing flowers crowned the confection.

I put down the chalks with a sigh. "Come see. It's done." I said.

She quickly ran forward and looked at my finished drawing. "Oh, Georgia! You have made me look beautiful!" she breathed.

"That's because you are, silly!" I laughed.

She blushed and shook her head but said, "I can see now that Mama was right in selecting this dress for me! How foolish I was to protest I did not like it just because of its color! And you have put my hair up. I shall ask Mama if I can put it up in precisely the same way."

"I am glad you like my portrait of you," I said. "You may keep it if you wish."

"Oh, may I? Dear Georgia, you are too kind!" She cast her arms around me in a fervent hug.

"Watch yourself!" I exclaimed, and laughed at her enthusiasm. "You have chalk dust on your dress!" She backed away, brushing at a white streak with her hand. "Of course you may have it! How else are you going to remember how you will put up your hair?"

"I will show it to Mama as soon as I get home!"

promised Samantha. We did not talk long after this, for I was flattered to see she was eager to take my portrait home to show Lady Ashcombe.

The last fitting was the day before the party. I stood on a stool while Miss Barton pinned my dress here and there and Mama looked on. It took too long, I thought, and I itched frequently and was pricked by pins more times than I could count. Miss Barton finally stood back to view her handiwork. "How does it fit?" asked Mama.

"It is a little tight in the bodice front," I said.

"Can you raise your arms properly?" asked Miss Barton.

I raised them gingerly and found the tightness did not restrict their movement at all. "Yes, quite well."

"We needn't worry about it, then," replied Mama. "The neckline is high enough to make it of no matter." Miss Barton nodded in agreement. Much to my relief, I was soon unpinned and released to put on my usual day dress.

I was almost in alt as the next afternoon crept to a close. As Grimley brushed and styled my hair, I could see in the mirror that my cheeks had a glowing blush that swept up almost to my temples. For the first time, I was to have my hair put up just as Mama had hers—no schoolgirlish crown of braids, but as sophisticated as anything that might be found in a fashion plate. I wondered if Lucas and Samantha would recognize me with it styled in the simple knot atop my head and the little curls Grimley had managed to coax out to frame my face. I was ready to put on my new dress.

Mama's abigail carefully lifted the dress over my head and gently pulled it on. As she laced up the back, I looked down to smooth the skirt. My heart stopped. "Oh, nooo!" I wailed.

Grimley stopped lacing and swiftly came to face me. "What is wrong, miss?" she said, looking over me anxiously.

The neckline was a full four inches below what it had been earlier that morning. The tight bodice was of no help, either; it pushed my bosom a little upward so that it seemed more full than it was. I looked, I thought, as if I were a misprint in Ackermann's! The ruffles, which I thought added interest to the high cut, now brought full attention to a line that was not more, I was sure, than an inch and a half from the crest of my bosom.

Grimley was still worriedly searching my person with her eyes, apparently finding nothing wrong. "Miss Georgia, I don't see—"

"My *bosom*!" I shouted. "My *bosom* is going to *fall* out of this *dress*!"

Grimley pressed her hands to her ears. "No need to raise your voice, I'm sure!" she said testily. "It's not like I've grown deaf!" She stepped back, arms akimbo, to survey the wanton piece of cloth I had on. "You look very well, if I may say so, miss, as a young lady should. I'll not say I wasn't glad to hear you changed your mind about that neckline, Miss Georgia, for those ruffles near your chin would have been the ruination of that dress, if truth be told!"

"Changed my mind! I did *not* change my mind! Where did you hear—"

"Georgia! You look charming, my dear," exclaimed Mama as she swept in the room. "Ah, let me look at you!" She walked around me appreciatively. "Oh, to think my little girl has grown up so quickly! And into such a lovely young lady!" Her voice trembled sentimentally, and Grimley gave her a handkerchief with which Mama dabbed at a tear. "Why, I can remember—"

"Mother!" I said in warning. "I cannot wear this dress to Samantha's party." I looked into the mirror. The dress was net over silk satin, and I had thought when we bought it that with two fabrics combined, I would be well covered. But the net was sheer, the cut was close, and the light blue silk shimmered slightly underneath when it clung briefly to my form and whispered softly when it released. It looked as if I were walking through water when I moved. Surely, I thought, my form is just as revealed in this dress as it would be underwater!

Mama raised her brows in surprise. "Whyever can you not wear it, darling? It is a lovely dress, so particularly suited to you!"

I blushed. "Why, why, look at it!" I exclaimed.

"So?" replied Mama after looking me up and down.

I closed my eyes for a moment and counted to ten. I pointed to my chest. "I *bulge!*"

"Mountains out of molehills, my dear!" said Mama, and laughed at her own quip. I did not. It did not seem to me to be a laughing matter.

"I am going to *fall* out of this dress!" I persisted.

"No, you are not. See these tucks in the cloth? It may make the bodice seem tight, but it also prevents anything being out of order. One of the secrets of dressmaking!"

"The one, no doubt, that we are not supposed to tell gentlemen," I replied sarcastically.

"Really, Georgia!" Mama tried to sound affronted, but she turned and I could see her giggling behind her hand. She was still laughing at her quip. Grimley eyed her disapprovingly and looked pointedly at the ormolu clock on the mantelpiece. "Oh, yes, the time!" Mama wiped the smile off her face—unsuccessfully. "You need only pull up your underdress a bit above the edge of your bodice and you will be done dressing. It is getting late, so you must hurry!" She left the room, shoulders shaking with scarcely suppressed laughter.

6

I had no choice but to wear the dress as it was. I had no other suitable gown with which to attend Samantha's party. I tried at first to put a lace fichu around my neck to hide the offending bulges, but Grimley quickly whipped it off from behind. *"If,* miss, you think to leave this house so you can inform both great and small that *I* am a person who delights in dressing her ladies like *dowds,* you are mightily mistaken! *I* have my reputation to think of, miss, if you do not!" She put a small pearl pendant around my neck instead. It nestled between and a little above the bulges.

I was pushed into the carriage and onto the seat. I looked at Betty, the scullery maid, who was the only servant who could be spared from her duties to accompany me. She sneezed. For a moment I envied her. *She* did not have to worry about exposing herself to all and sundry. All she had was a cold. Then I castigated myself for my selfishness. Betty would have to attend me even though she had a miserable cold, while all I had to do was enjoy myself—or try to. I lifted my chin firmly. I would insist she go home to rest. Surely another, stouter servant would be available to accompany me home from Samantha's party later.

As the carriage slowed in front of the Ashcombe residence, however, I could not help thinking of my predicament. I motioned Betsy to get back into the carriage. While instructing the groom to take her home, I wondered miserably if I could claim susceptibility to chills so I could keep my cloak on.

The hope was futile. As I stepped into the Ashcombe residence, I saw the brightly lit fires in the hearth and felt the warmth permeating the merino wool. It helped nothing to see that the Ashcombes' house was far more spacious and richly decorated than mine. I knew Mama had to practice a few economies, but we lived comfortably and could occasionally indulge ourselves if we were careful. But here, when I looked at the elegantly furnished foyer and the rich carpets, I felt quite out of place. A footman came forward to take my cloak. "Miss . . . ?" he queried.

I put my hands on my cloak's collar, but the footman must have interpreted my motion to mean for him to remove it. He reached to take it.

"M-Miss Georgia C-Canning," I stammered, having to wrestle a bit in my attempt at retaining my cloak. "Perhaps I could—"

"Georgia!" cried Lucas's welcoming voice from the doorway, startling me so that I lost my hold on the collar. "Samantha will be glad to know you are here!" As he walked up to me, the cloak fell from my shoulders. His gaze fell from my face to my neck, and his jaw dropped slightly. He did not seem to be able to look very far past the pearl at the end of my necklace, and it seemed as if he were holding his breath. It was too late to try to seize my cloak, for the footman had already left, and I flushed hot and cold and hot again in embarrassment. I tried hunching my shoulders to disguise whatever I could, but this only made the situation worse, for the bodice front gaped open a little at the movement, and I distinctly felt the pearl roll about in the valley. I hastily straightened my shoulders.

A slow smile formed on Lucas's lips, and his eyes seemed a very deep blue as he looked into my own. He took my hand to his lips. "You look quite—quite grown-up," he said huskily. "Quite the lady! Very—"

"Lovely, wouldn't you say, Lucas?" came Samantha's voice as she floated up to us in her rose-and-white confection of a dress. I drew a sigh of relief. I did not know how to react to Lucas's hand kiss, and Samantha's entrance excused me from having to do so.

He cleared his throat. "Yes, quite the thing, I was going to say."

"Is that all?" cried Samantha. She looked from me to her brother, and an indecipherable expression passed over her face. She continued smoothly: "She looks beautiful! Georgia, you should always wear that shade of blue. It truly becomes you."

I recovered under her chatter. "Not always!" I laughed. "It would become quite tiresome forever to wear blue, I am sure! But come, let me look at you!"

I stepped back to view her in toto. Samantha looked almost exactly as I had imagined she would when I drew her in pastel chalk; she had even put up her hair in the way I had drawn it. The pink bodice gave a glowing, rosy cast to her normally pale skin, and the very high waist made her seem taller. The only difference was that my drawing didn't seem to reveal as much as the actual dress did. I surreptitiously compared her bodice with mine and found they were essentially of the same cut, though perhaps I protruded a little more than she. Not much more, thank God.

"Oh, you are just as I imagined you would look!" I said warmly. "You are beautiful, too, Samantha!" She blushed, shaking her head, and smiled.

Lucas cleared his throat again. "Well, now that you've both done the pretty, shall we go into the drawing room?" He gave both his arms to us, and we were escorted in what I thought was fine style.

I saw, as we entered the room, that there were only a few others there; I had come earlier than most. I felt nervous, for I knew only Lucas and

Samantha. "Oh, there's Mama," said Samantha, directing my gaze to a lady sitting by the pianoforte. She cast a glance at her brother before saying, "Oh, dear! I think I hear some others at the door! Lucas, do introduce Georgia to Mama; I shall be back shortly!" She hurried from us to the door.

I felt confused. I was sure that Samantha was going to introduce me to Lady Ashcombe, but she had relegated the task to her brother; this was more what Mama had envisioned than what I had expected. Of course, Samantha could not neglect her other guests. I looked up at Lucas uncertainly and saw that he was looking rather slack-jawed at his sister's retreating back. "Your mother knows, of course, that both you and Samantha are my good friends, does she not?"

He brightened. "Of course she does! Samantha never stops chattering about you, you know. M'mater must have heard your name a tedious number of times."

This was not at all heartening, for I did not want to be tedious even before I met Lady Ashcombe. Fortunately, I was not allowed to dwell on this, for he brought me immediately to his mother.

Her ladyship was a plump, comfortable woman. She, too, had the raven-black hair, but there was a swath of grey at one temple, which I thought looked quite distinguished. Her nose was less aquiline than Lucas's, but not as straight as Samantha's, and her kindly eyes were the same deep blue of her son's. "Mama, this is Miss Georgia

Canning. Miss Canning, my mother, Lady Ashcombe."

I curtsied and clasped my hands in front of me. "I am pleased to meet you, my lady," I said politely.

"And I you," returned Lady Ashcombe, smiling. She patted the settee beside her, "Come, sit beside me. I have heard much of you from Samantha." She gave a quick glance at her son. "And from Lucas. Lucas, dear, do go and fetch us some lemonade, if you please!" He obediently left. She turned back to me. "Now we can have a comfortable coze! Are you related to the Somerset Cannings?"

I wrinkled my brow. "I think so," I replied. "My father was the third son of the Viscount Canning. They live near Shepton Mallet, I believe."

Lady Ashcombe smiled and pressed my hand. "Ah, he distinguished himself under Wellington, did he not? You must be proud of your father! He did well for himself in the army. My husband, the late Lord Ashcombe, used to speak of him in his dispatches."

My heart warmed toward her, and I grew more optimistic for Mama. Miss Angstead had been right in saying my father's lineage and valor in battle could help make things right with society. I smiled gratefully at her. "My father fell in battle when I was quite young, but my mother has often shown me his portrait and told me of him, so yes, I am proud to be his daughter. I know he must have been a very good man."

Lady Ashcombe nodded in approval. "Indeed!

And speaking of portraits, I see you are an artist."
She gestured toward Samantha, who was talking
to a young man at the other end of the room.
"You see, we have copied the coiffure from your
drawing."

I blushed and cast my eyes downward, for I felt
suddenly shy at her compliment. "I—I thank you,
my lady, but I am the veriest amateur! I need far
more practice before I become truly proficient."

"Well, I must tell you that you have had your
first piece hung, for we have framed your pastel
picture and are displaying it in the parlour. A
good likeness, I think!"

"I am happy you think so, my lady. It gives me
hope that with practice I will be able to truly
wear the name of artist."

Lady Ashcombe raised her eyebrows. "You
plan to be an artist, then? Yes, I believe Samantha
has told me about your ambitions; it is no wonder she had taken a liking to you! She, too, has
ambitions." She smiled indulgently. "A thing I
believe will not hold her interest long when
eligible young men start calling."

I didn't want to be impertinent, so I said cautiously: "I think there are some ladies who are
authoresses even though they are married. Mrs.
Radcliffe, for example. Perhaps Samantha will be
like her."

"Hmmm." Lady Ashcombe frowned in thought,
then her face cleared. "No matter, as long as she
marries well, and happily." She sighed. "I do not
know that I want it spread about that Samantha
has literary leanings, however."

I felt a little disappointed that Lady Ashcombe would think this. With such enlightened and intelligent progeny as Lucas and Samantha, I thought she would think differently. But I saw that her precepts were not much different from Mama's. I could not see how Samantha's talent could make her any less beautiful or amiable, but I said: "I would think that Samantha's intelligence would be an asset rather than a detriment to a husband, would it not?"

Her ladyship smiled at my naiveté. "Bless you, child, for your loyalty, but you must know it is not always the case! Quite the contrary. My daughter's intelligence narrows the field considerably! Most men find it difficult to fathom the complex ways of a woman's mind in the first place, and this makes them feel quite nervous. Let them know there is a woman whose mind is as sharp as or sharper than a man's, and you will see them fleeing in droves from her!"

I felt somewhat disheartened. I knew I read more books than most of the girls in Miss Angstead's, so I must be in the same situation as Samantha—no, worse, for certainly my chestnut-colored hair was not à la mode as my friend's raven-black was. This seemed to narrow my options for my future, but I bolstered my courage with the knowledge that I was already practicing my painting.

Lady Ashcombe must have noticed my deflated look, for she said, "There are still many men, however, who appreciate wit and intelligence in a woman. And not clergymen, either!" she said when I looked skeptical. "Why, look at Lucas! I know someday he will be setting up a nursery, and *he* has no intentions toward being a clergyman, yet he is quite an intelligent young man. I am sure there are others who are superior in their understanding as well."

"Yes, he *is* intelligent, isn't he? I doubt there are others as gifted as he is," I said loyally.

She lifted her chin proudly but said with a twinkle, "I hope you will excuse a mother's pride, my dear, when I say I agree with you. Nevertheless, in all fairness I would say that most mothers would say so of a son who passed his examinations so easily."

"Oh, no! I am sure you do not exaggerate, my lady! I do not think there is anyone like Lord Ashcombe!" I said earnestly. She raised her brows questioningly. I blushed, for I did not mean to sound so impetuous. "What I mean is, I do not know anyone who has the talent he has. Why, to be able to remember verbatim everything he reads! Perfectly and in one reading! It is a wonderful gift. I wish *I* could do so."

She looked at me keenly. "So he told you that, did he? He is not wont to say much of it."

I nodded. "Yes, I know. He is very modest, I think, though he calls it common sense and good ton. I do not know much about society, but I can see what he means when he says puffing off one's virtues and abilities unwisely can get one in trouble. He explained to me about Oxford, you see," I said confidently, "And I know better about how to go on now. Well, perhaps not all about it," I amended.

Lady Ashcombe laughed. "I promise you there is more to it than that! My, it does seem Lucas has been confiding in you quite a bit—quite unlike him, I must say!" She gazed at me speculatively.

I recognized this as a look very similar to the ones Mama had been giving to Lucas when she found him in my company. I said hastily, "Oh, we are all comfortable friends—Samantha, Lucas, and I—I daresay he is merely grateful to me for getting him out of a fix."

"A fix?"

"Well . . . well, about four months ago, he fancied he was in love with my mother—Mama is very beautiful, you see—and she did not want to hurt him by turning him away, so I solved the problem for both of them by pointing out to him all the disadvantages of marrying her."

Lady Ashcombe's countenance was serene, but I could see amusement sparkling in her eye. "Such as...?" she prompted.

"I told him he would then be my steppapa, and he didn't quite seem to know what to do with the idea," I blurted.

Her shoulders shook for a moment, but she said, "I am disappointed. I had thought my son more resourceful than that. Did he not come up with a solution to this dilemma?"

I knit my brows for a second. "Oh, I remember! He said I could stay at his estates, but I said Mama would not consent because she is very much attached to me and would not want me out of her sight, especially since I had come home ill from school."

She threw back her head and laughed. "Thoroughly routed! What a grave disappointment for him it was, to be sure!"

I laughed back, saying, "No, indeed! I do believe he was even somewhat relieved!"

"Who was relieved?" came Lucas's voice from behind me.

I turned quickly around, blushing, but Lady Ashcombe said, "*I* am relieved you have finally come back with the lemonade! I was becoming thirsty, for it is quite warm."

"I would have come back sooner," Lucas said apologetically, "but there's quite a crush around the bowl." He gave us our glasses. I smiled at him and sipped my drink gratefully. He was gazing at me intently but, at my smile, grinned. "Enjoying yourself, then?"

I nodded. "Oh, yes!" I shifted on my seat. I felt strangely uncomfortable in his presence, a feeling I did not like, for it was quite different from the easy camaraderie he, Samantha, and I shared before. I suppose it was due to our encounter in the foyer when I first came; indeed, my feelings seemed to be softer echoes of that overwhelming embarrassment about my dress, and the hot-and-cold flashes had resolved themselves into a sensitive tingling across my skin. There was a tightness at the pit of my stomach, making me breathless.

It was as if he were looking at me differently, too; when our eyes met, he seemed to gaze into mine longer than was necessary, and I felt I had to look away first. Then, when I looked up again, I found him glancing away from me, as if not wanting to be caught staring. I wished he would stop, for it seemed quite unlike him. I wished *I* would stop, for I was feeling quite unlike *me*.

I looked about me and noticed the room had become more filled with guests, and I felt more nervous. The thought impressed itself forcefully upon me that, except for Lucas, Samantha, and now Lady Ashcombe, everyone was a stranger to me.

Lady Ashcombe must have noticed my anxious look, for she said kindly, "We have a few more guests than we did at the beginning of our talk, do we not? I must have Samantha introduce you to them."

Lucas must have noticed my anxiety as well, for he said gallantly, "Or I."

His mother glanced at my face and then gazed thoughtfully at her son. An amused look crossed her face before she said, "It is very kind of you, Lucas, to offer, and normally I would let you do so. However, I did set up this party for Samantha's benefit and to further her experience in social graces, so I will have her introduce Miss Canning to the rest of our guests."

Lucas looked disappointed, and a warmth seemed to spread where the tightness had been in my stomach, and I smiled at him. "I shall be all right, Lucas. Samantha has said there shall be dancing later. I do not know how to dance all the dances, but perhaps you could stand up with me on the ones I can."

Lady Ashcombe nodded approvingly. "Very

prettily said. You shall do well in your come-out someday, I think." She caught Samantha's eye and beckoned to her.

Samantha introduced me to her guests, and I am afraid that between my nervousness and concern that I remember everyone presented to me, I remembered very few. Most of the people present were children or grandchildren of Lady Ashcombe's friends and relations. Keeping in mind that this affair was to be a chance to practice society ways, I took note of what seemed pleasing in a person and what was not.

Samantha's demeanor was a model for me in that respect. I saw that her looks and liveliness combined to make her especially attractive not only to the young gentlemen in the party, but also to the young ladies. As she introduced me to all of her guests, I noted how many a gentleman's eye would brighten at her presence and how a shy wallflower would bloom when sprinkled with her light, pretty compliments. I resolved to copy her manner, although in my shyness among strangers I felt I had more in common with the wallflowers than with anyone else.

Dancing was suggested, and Lady Ashcombe volunteered to play the pianoforte only with the stipulation that those who could play the instrument take turns relieving her of the duty. The first dance was a country dance, and since I knew the steps, I stood up with a rather awkward-looking, inarticulate young man who executed each step surprisingly well. Samantha, as was proper, was led out into the dance by her brother. Lady Ashcombe gave the pianoforte up after three pieces, then Samantha took over playing some quadrilles.

With each dance the gathering grew more merry, and formal postures relaxed into ones of ease or excitement. I danced a country dance with Lucas, and caught up in the music, I felt more comfortable and was truly enjoying myself. I gaily volunteered when Samantha finished, and caught up in the gaiety of the evening, I immediately fell into a piece by Herr van Beethoven.

It was a few moments before I realized that the room had gone silent. I faltered and stopped and looked around. At least a double dozen eyes were either staring at me with accompanying open mouths or looking away with associated blushes. A fiery lump grew in my throat. I flushed and stammered, "I—I, what did I do? I know I am a little rusty, but—"

Samantha came up to me and laid a reassuring hand on my shoulder. "It's all right, Georgia. It is just that you played so beautifully, we didn't realize at first that you were playing a waltz." I looked at her blankly. She smiled. "You see, one is not allowed to dance the waltz unless one has been approved by the patronesses at Almack's." She looked at her mother. "Although I have never seen the sense in it; how are you to know how to dance it at Almack's if you haven't danced it before?"

Lady Ashcombe looked stern, but there was a twinkle in her eye. "No one, my dear, goes against what *those* august ladies say! It would be social ruin! However"—her face broke out in a smile—

"since this is *not* Almack's and since none of the patronesses are here, I do not see why we cannot practice it so that we all can do it when it *is* approved."

Samantha's face changed from a slightly shocked expression to one of joy. "Oh, Mama! You're, you're—a great gun!"

"Samantha!" Lady Ashcombe said reprovingly.

"As Lucas would say!" her daughter amended hastily.

Lucas turned toward her indignantly and said, "Not that you should be repeating such things even if I do say them!"

"My dears, please!" admonished Lady Ashcombe. She turned to me. "Please, do continue. You play extremely well; that piece was by Herr van Beethoven, was it not? I believe I recognize the style." I turned, relieved, back to the pianoforte.

Once again I was swept into the music, only vaguely aware of the other guests waltzing or attempting to do so. I do not see myself as a person of excessive sensibility; I do not faint or weep as young ladies are supposed to do when under extreme straits. But there is something about music that I cannot describe; I have found that it banishes for a time any worry or care I might have.

I felt the music, light and pleasant, coursing up my arms and, it seemed, through my heart. I felt a presence by my side, and I looked up to see Lucas standing there, smiling. Unhesitating and as unconstrained as the music, I smiled back at him. How wonderful it is, I thought, to have such good friends! His smile faded somewhat, but his eyes grew warmer, and as I reached up to turn the page of the music, he forestalled me and turned it himself.

At last I concluded the piece with a triumphant flourish. There was spontaneous clapping, and Lucas gave me his hand as I rose from the pianoforte, gaily curtsying and laughing.

Lucas motioned to Samantha to come to the pianoforte again. "Now it is your turn to waltz," his sister cried, and promptly sat down to play another lilting melody.

My discomfort returned. I looked around the room, and it seemed to me everyone was dancing much too close to each other. "I—I really don't know how to waltz. Perhaps—"

"Don't worry," Samantha said sunnily as her fingers danced across the keyboard. "Lucas does. He shall teach you."

I cast a look of alarm at him. "Easiest thing in the world," he assured me. "Here, give me your hand."

I blushed and turned my eyes away from him as he clasped me around the waist; I felt I could not look at him and in desperation glanced about the room for Lady Ashcombe. I found her looking at us, and upon catching her eye, she smiled and nodded. I felt trapped. Unless I wanted to be rude, I had to try to dance.

I moved stiffly, and in an effort to maintain a modest distance I stepped on his foot. "Here, now! You can't go about stepping on people's toes!" he exclaimed sternly. He released me, rubbing his chin thoughtfully. "All right. Try this: You're very good at playing the music with your fingers; try playing the rhythm with your feet. One-two-three, one-two-three. You see?" He whirled with an imaginary partner as I watched his feet. "Now, I am going to be pulling at you when we dance. That means I want you to go in the direction I am pulling you."

I glanced surreptitiously at the other guests and found to my relief that many of them, also, were learning how to dance.

"What if I want to go in another direction?" I argued.

"Not done," he returned unequivocally.

"Why not?" I said with a bit more heat.

"Too confusing having two people tugging at each other across the floor. That's what makes 'em step on each other's feet. Besides, even if it *were* done, you aren't well enough acquainted with the dance to do it." I had to agree with at least this last point whether I liked it or not—there was no escaping truth. I grudgingly nodded.

I felt more at ease in his arms this time. This was a dancing lesson, not a public embrace; it was impossible to forget this fact when one's partner would murmur sharp commands on where to place one's feet and admonishments not to tread on his toes again. This was the Lucas I knew, not the stranger who gazed at me warmly and kissed my hand as he murmured compliments I felt should not be mine.

"That's it! I thought you'd come around once I pointed out it wasn't much different from piano playing. Simpler, in fact." He grinned at me. I looked up at him briefly, murmuring my thanks, and feeling my feet go slightly awry, I looked down again. "Now the next thing you have to learn is not to look at your feet all the time so that you can flirt and engage in sparkling conversation with your partner."

I could almost waltz now without thinking about it—it *was* getting easier! "I don't flirt, and I don't know any sparkling conversation," I said firmly.

"Well, I agreed to help you out, didn't I?" he returned cheerfully. "You'll learn."

"But I don't want to fl—"

"Ah, Miss Canning, your eyes are twin stars fallen from heaven, your lips the rain-kissed petals of a rose—"

"Lucas, please don't!" I pleaded, my heart hammering. My gaze rose from the floor to his face, for his voice sounded too sincere for comfort. To my indignation, I saw he was laughing at me. "Why, you—!"

"Now, now! Pot calling the kettle black, you know. I can play-act as well as you can, you see!"

"Is *that* all it was!"

"But stay, my heart! Does Miss Canning care if I am sincere or not? Each word that falls from her lips is a die that determines the fortunes of my heart," he declaimed theatrically.

"Oh, stop it!" I exclaimed. "You know full well that any future connection between us is all in Mama's head, so I wasn't piqued at all. I was—was merely relieved that you *were* play-acting and not serious."

He still smiled, but an intent look grew in his eyes as he gazed at me. I looked away. He said lightly, "I see you aren't in the way of things yet. Not the sort of thing you should say to a gentleman when he douses you with flowery compliments. A little flirting, a little modest disclaiming, is the answer to it all, you see."

"I don't see how—I don't want to lead anyone to think—" I broke off in confusion.

"Not going to, if you do the thing correctly," he replied.

"But flirting—! The schoolmistresses at Miss Angstead's discourage it, you know."

He rolled his eyes. "Schoolmistresses! That's all very well if you are at school! No use for it there. I suppose I should really have said judicious flirting," he reflected as I gazed at him through my lashes. "Don't want to be thought fast, but you don't want to look as if you're going to be giving every man who admires you a rude set-down, either."

"It doesn't sound any different from walking the tightrope at Astley's Amphitheatre," I grumbled.

"It's easier than that—promise!" The music ended, and Lucas led me from the floor. He stopped by the sideboard to give me a glass of lemonade, then led me to a seat. "Thing is, you need to know how to deal with compliments—and set-downs, too. Tell me, what would you do if some young buck came up and said your eyes struck him to the heart with Cupid's arrow, and that he came back for you to pluck it out?"

"I'd tell him not to be so silly," I said testily.

Lucas shook his head. "If you liked the fellow, you might just give him the impression you didn't, especially in that tone of voice." He gave me a keen glance. "You might have lost the opportunity to make a friend."

I considered this. I conceded it would be agreeable to have more friends like Lucas and Samantha, and to turn away someone like them would be a sorry thing indeed. "Well then, what should I say?"

Lucas thought about this for a moment and absently sipped the lemonade from his glass. He immediately held it away from him and made a face. "Good God, why in the world did you let me drink this stuff?"

"I didn't!" I retorted. "You picked up a glass for yourself when you gave me one. It's lemonade," I added helpfully.

"Dashed well know what it is!" he said. "Can't stand the stuff."

"You're the one who picked it up," I said reasonably. "I did not know you hated it or I would have said something. Why did you?"

"Too busy talking with you, that's why!"

I fluttered my lashes at him. "Oh, Lord Ashcombe! I never thought my presence would distract you from your surroundings! If I had known, I assure you I would have put more of a distance between us!" I lowered my head modestly and peeked up through my lashes at him, daring him to laugh.

"So you *can* flirt!" he said wryly.

I raised my eyebrows at him. "You mean fluttering my eyelashes and all that sort of thing? Why, I was only funning!"

He grinned. "You would be," he said. "But it's what I meant about dealing with compliments in the right way. If you want to encourage a fellow's attentions, you do just what you did just now. He might come up with another compliment. I'm not sure how to turn off one, though." He considered this problem. "Samantha might be able to tell you how. She's had a few admirers already," he said proudly.

I could see that this must be true. Her fashionable loveliness was sure to win suitors, and her manners were neither too forward nor too aloof. "I suppose I should ask Samantha, then, for she seems to know how to get on very well," I commented, watching her chattering merrily to a tall young blond man by the pianoforte. "*Then* I shall really know how to get on in the world."

Lucas held up a hand. "Not even then, I'm afraid."

"There is more?" I exclaimed.

"Afraid so. All sorts of pitfalls for the unwary," he replied knowledgeably. "Fortune hunters, rakes, et cetera."

"Well, I won't have to worry about fortune hunters, as I only have a respectable portion. So I suppose I shall have to watch out for rakes. Why are they so objectionable?"

"Seducers," he replied, casting me a dark glance. "Trifling with a lady's affections without meaning anything serious."

I thought about this. "But Lucas, you said Sir

Jeremy was a rake, and *he* has serious intentions toward Mama. And he is a very good sort of gentleman, too," I concluded loyally. "Indeed, if all rakes are like Sir Jeremy, I shouldn't mind marrying one myself."

Lucas turned red about the ears. "I never said Sir Jeremy was a rake!" he protested.

"You certainly did! It was when you were in love with Mama and found she had gone out with him in his curricle!"

"Ah, well, caught up in the passion of the moment," he said, having the grace to blush. "No doubt I said any assortment of wild things I shouldn't have. Infatuated with your mother, you see."

"Yes, I know." I sighed. "Most men react that way when they see her. They can't help it, for she *is* beautiful."

He patted my hand. "You needn't worry. You're apt to rival her yourself by the time you're ready for your come-out," he said kindly. "In fact, you already—"

"Lucas, old boy! Can't keep all the ladies for yourself, you know!" cried a cheerful voice behind me. Lucas scowled briefly, and I turned to see a stocky young man as fair as Lucas was dark. "Give over now, cousin!" He grinned.

Lucas rose and introduced us—grudgingly, I thought. I looked at Sir Daniel Bassett and smiled.

I liked him immediately, for he had an open, jovial countenance, well tanned by the sun, and his blue-grey eyes were guileless. His eyes flickered over me in an appreciative way, and his expression seemed to grow warmer. I did not become alarmed as I had when Lucas did this, for I had come to the conclusion that perhaps this was the usual way that gentlemen behaved toward ladies at parties. An ethereal-looking blond girl sat herself down at the pianoforte and drew forth a tinkling melody. Sir Daniel seemed to prick up his ears at this and, after casting a mischievous look at Lucas, said: "How opportune! Miss Canning, if you would honor me with a dance?"

I glanced at Lucas and saw he looked a bit disgruntled. I would have liked continue our conversation but reflected that it would look quite particular if I refused Sir Daniel to sit with Lucas instead. Further, it would be quite impolite to Sir Daniel. I smiled at Lucas reassuringly and extended my hand to his cousin. "I would be delighted, sir." He threw a triumphant glance at Lucas, and we started on the steps of the dance.

I had a delightful, if energetic dance with Sir Daniel, and from him I passed to sundry other gentlemen. Occasionally, if I knew the steps of a dance fairly well, I would glance around to see how Samantha and her brother were doing. Samantha was usually surrounded by at least three or four young men, and at times I would see her cheeks flushing peach pink with enthusiasm or her eyes lighting in a smile. I would like to say that Lucas, too, was as animated, but when I caught sight of him, he had a bored look on his face despite the fact that the ethereal blonde had gravitated toward him after her musical performance and was casting languishing glances at him. I saw him dancing with her, and I think he danced a few times with some other very eager girls, but I did not notice all that much, as I was watching my feet and attempting to practice my flirting skills.

The evening passed more quickly than I thought it would at its outset. My shyness had fallen from me as I grew more comfortable with the friendly faces in Samantha's party—so different from what I had imagined it would be; indeed, a whole world away from Miss Angstead's Seminary. It was a puzzle to me how I could be treated one way at Miss Angstead's and a totally different way at the Ashcombes'. I didn't think on this long, however. Soon the guests were leaving, mostly in pairs, and the room grew more and more empty. I glanced at the clock on the mantelpiece, exclaimed at the lateness, and hastily went to take my leave of Lady Ashcombe.

"I am grateful you invited me," I said, curtsying to my hostess. "I've had such a delightful time. I don't know how to thank you!"

"Tish, child!" She waved her hand at my effusiveness. "We were most happy to have you. This is but a small affair for Samantha, nothing to be excited over. There shall be more, I assure you!"

I put my cloak on at the door, chatting all the while with Samantha. The footman opened the door, and to my dismay, I was greeted by a gust of rainy wind. I forgot that I had sent the carriage back with Betty and would have to wait until a message could be sent home to fetch me back. I did not look forward to the ride back, either; the carriage I came in had been a drafty thing. I hesitated. Perhaps I could ask for an umbrella and servant and then walk—it would take an hour and a half just to send home for the carriage, have it hitched and at the Ashcombes' door. By that time I would be at home if I walked. I turned to Samantha and asked for an umbrella and a footman or maid.

"But Georgia!" cried Samantha. "Surely you are not going out in that!"

I turned and smiled at her. "I don't know how else I am going to go home unless I step past this threshold."

"But it's raining dreadfully, and an umbrella would be almost useless! But wait! I shall order our own carriage." She left before I could protest.

Obediently I waited. The Ashcombes' coachmen were quick; I could hear their carriage draw up before twenty minutes passed. I wondered if a servant would fetch me out, but then Samantha came back with an umbrella and Lucas in tow. "Here, now!" she exclaimed. "Lucas shall escort you home and carry the umbrella for you."

"Really, Samantha!" I said hastily, "I shall do just fine with the umbrella. Lucas need not escort me at all."

"Not a problem, truly!" asserted Lucas, looking a little harassed nevertheless.

"Yes, and besides, your maid has gone, and you must have someone accompany you," added his sister. She looked at me earnestly. "We would not be doing our duty as hosts and would be quite put out if we didn't have you escorted home. It would be a terribly long time before your own carriage arrived here, and ours is already at the door—and you mustn't worry, for it is closed and will keep the weather out."

I had not thought of this, that weather and darkness would make a difference or that I would cause an inconvenience to my hosts by refusing, so I bowed to Samantha's superior knowledge of such things. I did not want to offend their sense of hospitality. I nodded then and took Lucas's offered arm. I turned one more time to wave good-bye to Samantha, and it seemed I surprised a smug look on her face before she smiled and waved back; there was no trace of it as we moved toward the carriage, however, so I dismissed it from my mind.

As we stepped out, Lucas let out an inarticulate noise that sounded suspiciously like an oath. "Samantha *would* order the wrong one! At least most of the repairs have been made on it. Well, it's too late to change, and I suppose we shall have to make do. Fortunately, it's in working condition."

I looked up to see that though the carriage was indeed closed, it was a small coach, and we would have to sit side by side in it. I cast a surreptitious look at Lucas. He looked quite put out.

"I do not mind it, Lucas, if you do not," I said hesitantly. I felt a little uncomfortable, but then, I did not know what to think of this new unease I had with him. It was the newness of the social experience, I told myself, and felt comforted. Lucas had been like a brother to me. Why should I feel uncomfortable?

Lucas looked down at me and smiled. "I don't," he said.

It was dim within, but the carriage lamps lighted it enough so that we could still see each other. I sighed happily as I sat down on the carriage seat. "Oh, Lucas, this party must be the best thing that has ever happened to me! I have never had such fun in all my life, I am sure! It was so kind in Samantha and your mother to invite me! Everyone I met seemed so agreeable, and everything so beautiful, too!"

Lucas shrugged. "It's all right, if you like such halfling affairs."

"I refuse to think it a bore, however unfashionable it may be! I liked it." I cast him a mischievous look. "Besides, I would hardly call Sir Daniel a halfling. He was very kind to me."

"You mean he flirted outrageously with you!" he retorted.

"But did you not say I ought to practice flirting, just to get in the way of things?"

"You were doing quite well by yourself, I think."

I wrinkled my brow. "But how can I do well by myself? I don't see how I could flirt alone."

"Oh, you know what I mean!" he said, then caught my eye. I grinned at him, and he returned it reluctantly. "Oh, I suppose Samantha's party wasn't so poor." He was silent for a while, then said proudly: "Samantha did very well, too, I think; not too bad looking, if I may say so."

"Oh, yes!" I exclaimed. "I was so flattered that Lady Ashcombe decided to copy my drawing of your sister's hair." I sighed. "Samantha is very beautiful."

"So are you," said Lucas.

I blushed lightly and laughed. "I thought you said that I only looked 'quite the thing.'"

"Nothing of the kind."

"What!" I sat up straight. "After Samantha came in, you said—"

"Oh, well, 'after Samantha came in'!" he said as if that event made all utterances thereafter null and void. "You must remember *before* she came in, I greeted you like this." He took my hand and kissed it, grinning. "Then I said, 'You look quite— quite grown-up.'" He drew closer, and I think I drew in my breath as he continued. "'Quite the lady! Very—'" He stopped, his grin fading, and stared into my eyes so long, I finally looked down into my lap. I felt a finger under my chin and was compelled to lift my eyes again to his; suddenly his face was closer than ever. "Lovely," he breathed, and I felt his lips on mine.

His mouth was as soft and light as butterfly's wings but grew more firm as I sat still, so very still. There was a strange tingly dizziness that flowed from the top of my head to the tips of my toes—rather like a muted and continuous version of the shock one gets after rubbing one's feet on a carpet. It seemed all I could do was close my eyes to keep the dizziness at bay.

How very odd it was, this kissing, and how new!
I was not sure if I liked it or not, for it made me
feel very strange. It had been cold in the carriage,
and now I felt quite warm, but Lucas's fingers, like
delicate feathers moving along the line of my
jawbone to my ear, made me shiver. A faint scent
of spice came to me—bay rum?—and I wished I
could catch that intriguing scent again. I was
curious. Perhaps . . . perhaps I would feel less
shivery if I moved toward him. . . . I tentatively put
my hand up to his cheek.

It was as if he read my thoughts, for I felt his
hand move to my waist and pull me closer. His
lips lifted slightly from mine, and he sighed,
"Lovely..." before he descended again, this time
missing my mouth altogether and moving toward
my ear—and down. The change did not matter in
the least, I noted hazily. I felt just as tingly, just as
warm and shivery as before.

It was not until a soft and delicate caress dis-
turbed the chain that held my pendant and
caused the pearl to roll that my senses returned. I
sat up in shock, pushing Lord Ashcombe forcibly
away.

I pressed myself against the side of the carriage
away from him, staring at him and breathing in
gasps. He, too, was staring at me and with an odd,
puzzled expression in his eyes, as if he were
wondering how I had come to sit across from him
in a carriage. I looked down, and to my alarm I
found my cloak had come undone.

I did not know what to think. I had thought of
Lucas as Mama's erstwhile and too youthful

admirer, then a friend, and Samantha's brother. Indeed, he had always acted as brotherly toward me as he had toward Samantha. But one does not kiss one's sister the way he kissed me, I felt sure, and this abrupt change of behavior—or was it so very abrupt?—frightened me a little. This evening had changed him—or perhaps it had changed me?

Now I saw how really foolish my ambitions to become a governess were. Indeed, Lucas was right. After all, if he, the brother of my friend, could not keep from kissing me, how would it be in a stranger's household with no friends or relations to watch over me? I remembered suddenly what Mama had once said about being alone with a man—that society would think wrongly of me because of it. Surely that was true, for some had thought it of Mama! Shame made my face warm—I should not have done this kissing, and curiosity was no excuse.

I glanced at Lucas. He still seemed bewildered, but a look of concern came over his face. He held out his hand to me. "Georgia—I am sorry. I did not mean—I should not have, well—Not that it wasn't—" He cleared his throat. "I mean to say—"

I still felt strange and breathless and trembling all at once. I tried to sit up straight, but my legs felt shaky, and it was awkward to push up with them. I fumbled against the side of the carriage for some purchase so as to straighten myself. My hand touched metal, and glad of some support, I leaned against it.

Alarm flashed across Lucas's face. "Georgia, don't—!"

Suddenly the carriage door flew open, rain slashed at my face, and thunder pounded through my head. I knew no more.

7

I awoke amidst a raging headache, my body was racked with pain, and I was hot and cold by turns. The doctor came, and I remembered hearing the words *concussion* and *influenza.* Soon the aches and dizziness faded; and Mama wept in relief to see that my illness was mild. However, I spent more time gazing out the window from my bed than making the effort to be up and doing. There was something so very comfortable about my bed with its white ruffles and blue-and-rose canopy, and my room felt especially warm and sheltering when I gazed out at London's offering of waterlogged clouds and dank fog. At times my room seemed to be a world unto itself, calm and peaceful, with Mama and Grimley its only other inhabitants, acting like slightly worried bees in an encompassing hive.

I did not remember entirely how I came home, but it apparently caused quite an uproar when Lord Ashcombe carried me in. I wondered briefly how he explained my state, then left the thought. Whatever it was, I would make clear that it was really my own foolishness. I tried to tell Mama so, but she only hushed me and said I could talk later. I was tired, and I ached, so I let it alone.

At first, with my initial listlessness, I acknowledged them as much as a queen bee would her helpers. As I healed, however, my youthful constitution demanded more activity—or perhaps Mama's anxious buzzing eventually wore through the thick coating I seemed to have on my nerves. But all at once it seemed she tucked the bedclothes about me and shifted my pillows once too often. "Mother, I am quite comfortable enough, if you please!" I snapped one afternoon.

She started and stepped back. "I am sorry, my dear! I was only looking to your comfort." To my surprise, she cast an anxious look at Sir Jeremy, who was the only visitor allowed me for the first two weeks of my convalescence. He only seemed to sit more firmly on the armchair by the window and cast me an amused look. It occurred to me that Mama of late had tried to keep Sir Jeremy and myself from meeting for any length of time—probably to keep us from verbal wrestling. I smiled as sweetly as I could at him and saw that Mama looked rather resigned.

"Dear Mama," I complained gently, "I do feel *so*

thirsty. Perhaps some lemonade . . . ? And please don't let Grimley make it; she makes it too weak." I smiled winningly at her. "I like the way *you* make it best." She eyed me warily for a moment, then sighed and left to get the lemonade.

I gazed at Sir Jeremy for a bit before saying in a conversational tone, "So, why haven't you married Mama yet?" I was not sure what made me take the direct route, for I delighted in Tactics and Strategy. I think it was because of the overwhelming tiredness and lethargy that had come over me during my convalescence and the frustration brought on by my own tortuous methods.

I finally admitted that to myself. It was a childish thing to have done; all this planning and scheming and imagining I could make all perfect by waving the wand of sheer will. And I was not a child anymore after all. I had gone to a dinner party with my hair up high and neckline low, and . . . and I had been kissed.

I blushed at that last thought and shivered and wondered if I was totally wanton and if it showed. Apparently, Sir Jeremy did not perceive my changed state, for he seemed to take my blush as relating to my bluntness and merely smiled. "It is customary, I think, to receive the lady's permission before one marries her," he replied. "I did ask, you know." His smile turned wry.

"So what of that?" I said testily, shifting my pillows. "You must know she loves you."

"Does she? That seems a strange reason for refusing me, don't you think? I am considered to be on the rakish side; a discreet friendship may

be more palatable to some than a public associa-
tion such as marriage. Perhaps that is the case
with your mother." He shrugged carelessly, but
his expression saddened and he turned to look
out the window.

I rolled my eyes at how silly some elders could
be (vowing that I would never be so), and I dived
into the bedcovers to stifle a chuckle—unsuccessfully. Sir Jeremy's eyes shot to mine as I peeped
out from behind the comforter. I unveiled my grin
and said, "If you must know, she refused you
because she thinks *she* is unworthy of *you*!"

A gleam sparked in his eye, but only briefly.
"Celia always did say you had a fine imagination,"
he replied.

"Not at all," I said promptly. "Mama told me so
before I came back from school."

"And why would she reveal anything of the sort
to you?"

A spark of anger flared within me, but I damped
it down. "I am not telling a falsehood," I said as
calmly as I could. "It's because I asked her. She's
been very lonely." I blushed.

I think my blush convinced him, for he nodded
and said: "She is a difficult woman to convince,
you know." He looked out at the fog again.

I sighed. "Yes, I know. She believes people think
she is not entirely respectable and that she would
ruin you by marrying you."

"Ha! The rich and rakish Sir Jeremy Swift?
Hardly." His hand gripped the arm of the chair,
then relaxed. "The invitations would flood my
house once I married. A married man"—he smiled

ironically—"being eminently more respectable than a bachelor."

"Exactly!" I exclaimed. "Only she does not see it that way. A tradesman's daughter, she says, shouldn't look as high as Sir Jeremy Swift, and if you don't know what is good for you, she does!"

He started and looked back at me from the window, brought back from his thoughts. "I shouldn't mention such disreputable things to you, my girl—you should have stopped me." He looked stern, but his eyes smiled.

"Oh, I don't mind," I said comfortably. "You are going to be my papa, after all."

He grinned in spite of himself. "And how am I going to do that, seeing that your dear mama refuses to marry me, stubborn woman that she is?"

"You shall abduct her, of course!" I said, hugging the comforter to me and bouncing gleefully in the bed.

I overheard once that a rake makes the most exacting of husbands and fathers; Sir Jeremy's eyes grew quite steely cold, and he told me to quit bouncing about like a hoyden, and that Mama had let me read too many novels. "Abduct her. Indeed. *Quite* a respectable way to become married," he said with a cool irony that made me quit bouncing and in fact made me shrink under the covers. I was also a little disappointed. I had always thought rakes would be quite innovative about getting reluctant ladies to do as they wished, but Sir Jeremy seemed sadly lacking in this skill.

"Well . . . well, Mama has a great deal of

sensibility, you know; she might have taken your acceptance of her refusal in the wrong way," I said tentatively.

"Oh?" he replied skeptically.

"She may think your lack of persistence in the matter means you agree with her conception of her place in society."

"Nonsense," replied Sir Jeremy. "She must know it is because I respect her wish not to marry me."

"You must admit that though Mama is very beautiful, she is not at all vain," I said. "She may not think it respect, but contempt for her social background."

Sir Jeremy's brows drew together in thought.

"Besides," I said earnestly, "you needn't really *abduct* her. I can imagine a nice day, fit for driving out to the country, a light luncheon packed away; and if a special license was *accidentally* packed in it, and if you just *happened* to view a quaint church with interesting architecture as well, I would think that one would be naturally *inclined* to go along with fate and have it done." I smiled hopefully at him. "Wouldn't you think so?"

"No," he said baldly, but he glanced once more at me before gazing out the window again, looking almost as if he were about to laugh. I began to argue with him, but Mama came in then with the lemonade. I settled into a depressed fog between sips, mentally cursing the stubborn, outright imperviousness of the older generation.

Mama's and Sir Jeremy's visit was over soon

enough, which was just as well, for I wanted to be alone. I let my eyes droop a few times, and Mama, ever vigilant, stood up decisively to ring for a maid to clear away the refreshment. Sir Jeremy made his excuses to leave. They went to the door at the same time, and he held it open for Mama. "I do not want to see your mother run ragged any more than she is now, so rest well, young lady," he admonished.

"Now, Jeremy!" said Mama as she stepped past him. He unceremoniously pushed her through, and before the door closed, he turned to me once more. "And I shall take care of the rest!" he said. A slim hand appeared around the door, pulling him out of sight and closing the door.

I could hear Mama's voice, scolding. "I must say, Jeremy, you act no differently from a little boy sometimes!"

I sank back into my pillows with a sigh and closed my eyes. Somehow, I fell asleep much faster than I had before.

The next few days saw the clouds drifting northward, for a fine south wind had sprung up and swept clean all the corners of London's cobwebby ceiling. Then flowers bloomed in my bedroom, for I was able to receive get-well gifts and then, finally, visitors.

I woke one morning to find Mama arranging flowers in a vase next to the bed. "Roses!" I exclaimed. The blooms were not large, but they were well formed and a deep pink color, fading to a lighter pink white at the petal edges. I knew they must have been hothouse roses, but they had a gentle, sweet scent nevertheless.

"From an admirer, love," replied Mama, her voice teasing. I looked carefully at her but said nothing, unwilling to guess who it was. She laid a card on my lap.

Opening it, I let out a breath I did not know I had been holding. "Oh, it's Sir Daniel Bassett," I said, and relaxed against the pillows. "He is related to the Ashcombes; I met him at Samantha's party."

Mama lifted an eyebrow. "He must have been quite taken with you to send roses."

I shrugged. "He was no more attentive to me than he was to Samantha. He is rather amusing, and flirts, but that is all." I looked around the room. "Did anything else come while I was asleep?"

"Greedy!" Mama reproved, but laughed. "Yes, two things. Samantha and Lord Ashcombe stopped by not three quarters of an hour ago. Here's the first." She handed me a brown package.

I opened the note attached to it. "It's from Samantha." I read the note. "'I hope you are getting well; Lucas and I shall visit again to make sure you are! As you might guess, the package contains a book. I hope you enjoy it as much as I did.'" I tore the brown wrapping in my haste to see the title, then lifted it reverently from the shreds. "Oh, Mama! It's *Pride and Prejudice*! Samantha must have remembered that I haven't read this yet." I eagerly but gently opened the front cover and started to read.

Her slim hand closed the book again. "Really,

my dear! You *do* have one more present, you know. You can read later."

"Is this from Samantha, too?" I asked, taking the slim package. Mama merely smiled. The brown wrapping covered a black box, and inside was a note atop a swath of tissue. I opened the note. "I deeply regret I distressed you so the night of Samantha's party," said the dark, angular writing. "It must have been the lemonade. I hope you will forgive me and allow me to pay my respects in person. Yr Obed. Serv't, Lucas Ashcombe." Lemonade! I thought to myself, and almost laughed, but a lump in my throat turned it into a wobbly smile instead. My hand was almost steady as I laid aside the tissue in the box and lifted out a delicate fan.

I spread apart the ivory sticks. Their bases were intricately carved, and a loop of tasseled silk was strung from them. The nine Muses were painted on the fan on a sylvan background. At one end of the row of Muses was Apollo playing his harp and Euterpe singing with it; on the other end was the god Pan playing his pipes with Terpsichore dancing gaily to its melody. Between them all were the rest of the Muses acting out their various chosen interests. I laid out the fan on my lap and stroked it outward, the better to see the whole. I felt a hand on my shoulder and looked up.

"It is very beautiful," said Mama. She raised her eyebrows in inquiry.

I looked away. "It is from Luc—Lord Ashcombe. I think it is beautiful, too," I said as matter-of-factly as I could.

"He must quite like you," Mama said carefully. I gave her a questioning glance. "He seems to have looked for a fan with great care and found one whose subject suits a learned young lady as yourself."

"We are all good friends," I said dully, still stroking the fan. Somehow, I did not want to think about anything right then. I folded it up again and put it back in the black box with the tissue. "I should write thank-you letters to all of them." I shifted in the bed and let my legs hang from the side of it, then slid off the bed. I padded to my writing desk, pulled out some letter paper, and started to trim my pen. After I had done my first letter to Sir Daniel, I stretched and looked around. Mama had left so quietly, I did not notice she was gone.

As I said, I had visitors after the possibility of infection from influenza passed. I was allowed to leave my bedroom and go downstairs in the sitting room or parlour as long as I kept to the chaise longue and laid a shawl on my lap. Some of my visitors were Mama's acquaintances, but to my surprise most were people I had met at the Ashcombes'. Among them was Sir Daniel, and I took the opportunity to thank him again for the roses.

"They were quite lovely," I said. He sat negligently on a footstool next to me.

"Not as lovely as their recipient," he returned, taking in my dishabille with a gleaming eye.

I blushed but said with spirit, "How can you say so, sir? The roses were a deep pink, and I am quite pale after my illness."

"A delicate sylph, touched with stars and moonlight," he replied soulfully. This was a bit much, I thought. As I was accustomed to robust good health and a certain roundedness to my figure, I had difficulty seeing myself in this light and raised a skeptical eyebrow.

"Quite," I said in a damping voice, and ignored Mama's frown. I turned the conversation—neatly, I thought, so Mama need not continue frowning—to other things, among them Samantha's party. We discussed the people there, and Sir Daniel related what he knew of them in his humorous way. The half hour went quickly, and then he began to take his leave. I petitioned him to call on Samantha to see how she did; though she had visited, I had been asleep and could not see her.

The response was quick; Samantha called on me two days after Sir Daniel did. "Samantha!" I cried as she was announced. I rang for refreshment, as Mama was not in the parlour with me. Sir Jeremy and I had argued with her vigorously, claiming I was quite well enough for her to leave my side so that he could show both Mama and his new phaeton off to the rest of London. After I assured Mama that I would leave a (very short) list of people who were allowed to call with the butler so that I would not become overtired with visitors, she agreed.

"Oh, Georgia, I am so sorry!" cried Samantha. She almost ran to where I reclined.

THE MARRIAGE SCHEME   147 ✦

"Why?" I asked, bewildered.

"It is all my fault!" she said, her eyes filling with tears. "I ordered the wrong carriage! I forgot that it was not wholly repaired—I thought the door was already mended."

"Please don't cry, Samantha! You could not have known! I seem to remember Lucas saying it was the wrong one, though. Did he scold you terribly for it?"

"Oh, no!" said Samantha. "That was what was so horrid. He was perfectly gentlemanly about it, and told me I couldn't have known, and that it really wasn't my fault at all! I felt such a wretch. I would much rather he had raked me over the coals! Oh, do say you forgive me, Georgia!"

I took her hands in mine. "Of course I shall! But you needn't be sorry. Lucas was quite right. You could not have known, and it is not your fault. It was just chance, I know." I smiled at her. "Besides, you must know how glad I am you came! You don't know how terribly bored I have been!"

Samantha smiled back, relieved. "What, with *Pride and Prejudice* to occupy you? I am surprised; I thought you would like that book."

"Oh, no, the book is wonderful. But that is *all* I have to do! Mama will not even let me do any mending."

She laughed and sat on a chair near me. "Poor honey! You *are* bored! I cannot imagine any other reason you would want to take on a task as horrid as mending!"

"Yes, and you should have seen Mama's face when I asked her for some!" I giggled. "She instantly ordered some cold cloths in case I should have been fevered!"

Samantha snuggled deeper in her chair. "*Are* you feeling better? You were asleep and quite poorly when last Lucas and I came calling."

"Oh, much! But Mama insists on keeping me in cotton-wool. It is always so when I am ill, even though the doctor says I have a very strong constitution." I paused, thinking. "I suppose it is because I am the only relation Mama has left, really. She would be very lonely without me."

"Not if she married again, as you are planning," she replied.

I looked down at my clasped hands on my lap. I felt a little uncomfortable—because I had not made much headway in that direction, I told myself—but nodded. "Yes, that's true. And perhaps she wouldn't be cosseting me so much if that happened."

"And then you could be free to do whatever it is you want to do with your life," she said cheerily. "Schoolteaching, painting, or, or—" She leaned forward on her chair and frowned briefly, chin in hand. "Whatever was it that we decided on for you, Georgia?"

For some reason I felt she was watching me carefully, but when I looked at her, she seemed all intent puzzlement. "I think it was painting," I said vaguely.

She smiled. "That's it." She sat back on the chair, and this time she did give me an intent glance. "If you don't become married, that is."

"Oh, well, one cannot always depend on getting

married, you know." Even to my own ears my voice sounded dull. Samantha looked concerned and came over to me to lay a hand on my forehead.

"You don't feel feverish. Are you sure you are feeling better?" Her brow creased anxiously.

"Now don't *you* try to put me in cotton-wool!" I exclaimed, and grinned.

She smiled back. "I promise I won't!"

We talked, then, of outings we would have when I was fully recovered, and I assured her I would be ready to go out in a few days. "It's a pity, but our coachman will have to drive us about." Samantha sighed after a pause. "I do like to watch Lucas drive, but it cannot be for a while."

I glanced at her quickly and looked down at my hands. "Oh, is—is Lucas not here, then?"

"No, he is not, confound him!" An indignant frown crossed her face. "Off to the country to see to some matters there, he says! Just when we were starting to have some fun!" She shrugged her shoulders then and sat back on the chair. "Oh, I suppose it's unavoidable. I think I heard something about our new bailiff cheating our tenants. Lucas mumbled something about estate matters when he was on the way out, but I did not hear what it was."

An icicle seemed to be forming at the pit of my stomach, and the room seemed to go out of kilter. I closed my eyes and drew my shawl closer to me.

"You *are* ill!" cried Samantha.

The room stilled, and I opened my eyes and saw she was at my side, patting and stroking my hand. I smiled weakly. "No, I'm well, truly. Just a small dizzy spell. I used to get them all the time right after my illness, but now they only come once in a great while. I'm well, really."

"Nevertheless, I am calling Miss Grimley. She did say you weren't to be having visitors for long, and I can see she was right. You should have told me you were feeling tired! I am not such a poor friend as to go boring on when you are ill! Now don't argue!" she said when I opened my mouth to protest. She summoned a maid to fetch Grimley.

"Doing more than she should, I'll be bound," Grimley remarked to no one in particular as she shut the door behind her. She glanced at the watch pinned at her bosom. "As I thought, miss. Two hours past luncheon and I do not think you have had your nap."

"I don't need a nap!" I said, indignant at being made to feel as if I were a child. I gazed at Samantha in appeal, but she only grinned.

"It's not that *I* would dictate to *you,* miss," Grimley said sternly, "but it's what the mistress ordered, and I have never done differently than what Miss Celia has said, though many's the time I've *thought* differently, *if* I may say so, miss."

Grimley was clearly determined to do Mama's bidding, and so, it seemed, was Samantha, for she pulled my shawl more closely around me and patted me on the back. "Now, Georgia, I see I have stayed much longer than I should have; I shall go now. Take care of yourself, and I shall call on you again later, when you are feeling more the thing."

"I *am* more the thing!" I said stubbornly, but was forestalled by Grimley, who pierced me with a gimlet eye.

"I have had, Miss Georgia, your bed prepared these two hours, as your mama wished," she said. "Far be it from me to disagree with you, miss, but it would break my heart to tell your mama—"

"For goodness' sakes, Grimley, leave be! I am *going*," I grumbled. I looked at Samantha, who was drawing on her gloves. "You shall visit again, soon, won't you?"

"Of course, silly!" Her grin turned mischievous as she went for the door. "*If* you promise to take your nap!"

"Why you—!" I threw a pillow at the closing door, while Grimley shook her head and clicked her tongue, herding me to my bedroom.

I was still grinning by the time I came to my room. I liked Samantha, but such a tease! Lucas could be like that, too. . . . An unfortunate thought. The grin was wiped from my mouth, for I felt the cold at the pit of my stomach again. I didn't want to think of him, and I had been successful so far, but I wasn't used to not thinking.

Stop thinking, stop thinking! I cried to myself. I pressed the palms of my hands to my eyes, as if I could blot out his image. But, of course, I could not. As I curled up on my bed and closed my eyes, his face came to me and I helplessly saw again his intelligent deep blue, black-fringed eyes, now laughing, now serious, now filled with that expression I did not know how to interpret. Last, but not least, I remembered the softness of his lips on mine and how I had let—no, wanted—him to kiss me in the carriage.

Shameless! My hands rose to cool my fiery cheeks at this thought, but some deep need fought my will and won the right to wander over that moment again. I searched for any tidbit of information that could tell me something, any-thing . . . anything about what I should do. My hand clenched into a fist and hit the pillows, and the rest of me followed soon after as I burst into tears.

Why couldn't things be the way they were before, with Samantha, Lucas, and me so comfort-ably friendly? Why did Lucas have to kiss me? *Why did you let him?* said a voice inside of me I couldn't ignore.

Perhaps, said the mocking little voice, *perhaps you are in love with him.*

This threw me into fresh tears; I realized it was more than "perhaps." I was not sure when it began; I saw I had not wanted to know, for it marked the ruin of all I had known before, all that was com-fortable and sure. For despite my scheming and planning, I was no closer to having Mama married than when first I came to London: both she and Sir Jeremy seemed as uncompromising as ever. *And you cannot leave her alone by herself,* cried another internal voice, though whether it was the voice of fear or love, I did not know. I only knew it sang a familiar refrain and meant no frightening changes—and thus was safe.

And Lucas, what of him? I was not so besotted or so stupid as to think that love on one side meant love on the other. Were not Mama's novels full of such examples of unrequited love? *But he kissed you!* reminded another voice within. *Could not that mean—?* But that comforting voice was cut off by the memory of Mama's unfortunate experience with a man who wanted to take advantage of her. He had even promised her marriage—but it was for naught; she discovered he was married already. She was lucky, she told me, that she had found out in time, before she had been totally compromised.

So what of Lucas? For all I knew, the kiss that turned my world top over tails meant nothing to him—perhaps he did not even care for it. Or if he did, my reaction to it in the carriage put paid to that. How could I have pushed him away from me as if he were odious? I cringed at what pain I might have inflicted on him—if he had cared for me. I thought, then, of the fan he gave me—surely that meant something? But again I recalled that Mama had received gifts long ago from that man who had not cared one whit for her. I wished there were a way I could know for sure—perhaps I dared ask him?

It struck me then that he was not present to ask. He had left London. "Off to the country to see to some matters there, he says!" Samantha had said, her voice as I remembered it tinged with skepticism. Perhaps, I reflected, he didn't want to be asked any such thing. Perhaps he didn't want to be bothered with any such awkward matters right now. Perhaps he didn't want to be bothered with *me*.

What conclusion did I come to? The safest, of

course. Above all things, I had always been proud of my mind and the force of will behind it, and I took refuge there once again. I resolutely wiped away my tears. The thing I must remember, I told myself sensibly, is that he had in no way made his intentions clear; whether he meant marriage or a carte blanche, as I remember it was called, I did not know. What was my station, after all? Lady Ashcombe might countenance me as a friend of her daughter's, but as a daughter-in-law? I did not know. Where was the line drawn? And would he not adopt the same attitudes as his mother? I argued to myself.

Above all, I would be safe; I did not want to be hurt as Mama had been hurt. The safest course, then, would be not to think of love or marriage at all, but to take comfort in what I had and knew. I would go on as I had before, caring for and being cared for by Mama, resolutely setting aside my feelings for Lucas, discarding my plans for her marriage with Sir Jeremy, since they did not seem to be working anyway. Who was I, after all, to fiddle with the destiny of others, whatever Miss Angstead might have thought?

I settled down more comfortably in the pillows. I had been foolish. I was only seventeen—well, almost eighteen, but I was not all *that* grown up. To be sure, I had gone to Samantha's party, wearing a far from schoolgirlish dress and my hair up, had been kissed— No, I would not think of that. After all, there were still more years to go before I would be absolutely on the shelf—if I considered marriage at all.

But Samantha is thinking of marriage and is of an age with you, whispered a last, fading voice. I ignored it. I started making other plans. Mama and I would be together, I would care for her, I would practice my painting until my pictures sold, I would . . . I finally fell into my despised nap.

I woke again to the sound of a light tapping. I rose up on my elbow, rubbing my eyes with one hand. "Yes? Who is it?" I said.

"It is I, Georgia," came Mama's voice. The door opened a crack, and she peered in. "Oh, dear, did I wake you? I had hoped I did not, but I could not wait to tell you." She floated to the window and swept aside the drapes. The sun shone on her hair and formed a halo about her face. "So dim in here! Oh, Georgia, I could not wait!" She turned to me, her face glowing, and clasped my hand in hers. "Oh, my dear girl, my dear, dear darling girl, I am to be married! I am so happy!"

8

My world turned top over tails again. I felt faint, but luckily Mama did not see this, for she had turned again to the window. Then she whirled around in an ecstatic waltz, laughing, and finally fell onto a chair. "Oh, I cannot believe it! Well, Jeremy had asked me before, and I had refused him since I did not believe he could seriously think my background would make me fit to be his wife. But, oh, my dear! He did think it! Why, he practically abducted me! I went out today thinking we were to have merely a small al fresco luncheon, and what should he do but pull a special license from the bread basket! And he had it arranged that we should be married in a quaint little church close by! Well, of course, I would not marry so abruptly, and I did want you there with me in church when we *did.* So we are to be married two weeks from now, in that same little church! You may imagine I could hardly eat after he pulled out the marriage license, but what is luncheon, after all, compared with marrying the man I love?"

I had recovered enough by this time to smile. "Oh, Mama, I am so glad," I said, determined to go through this without letting her know the turmoil I was in. "It is as I had hoped. I do like Sir Jeremy. It shall be nice to have a father again."

Perhaps my voice sounded odd, for Mama looked anxious and said, "Are—are you sure, my dear?" She looked almost like a child caught in a scrape, and this made me smile in spite of myself.

"Of course I am sure! Why, I have been scheming for you to marry Sir Jeremy since I came home! Clever, was I not, M-Mama?" I could not help myself; my voice broke and I sobbed unrestrainedly.

I felt comforting arms around me. "Oh, heavens, what have I done? I had thought you would have liked it; you did keep saying you wanted a father! I should never have succumbed to Jeremy's arguments!"

I lifted my head and summoned up a smile. "Nonsense, Mama! I am just so happy that you and Sir Jeremy will marry and that you shall not be lonely any longer. It is just this illness; I seem to succumb to the slightest sentimentalities!" I gave her a hug to reassure her—and myself. "I am so glad!" I put as much enthusiasm in my voice as I could. "Now I can be easy that you shall not be lonely again!"

She was convinced. Indeed, I *was* glad; how

could I not be when I could see her whole being shine with her love of Sir Jeremy? But...what of me? A selfish thought, but I could not help thinking it. It seemed that the base of my world was nothing but sand and my future unsure. I had pretended to think of myself finding employment and being Mama's sole support—but I more than half believed it myself. At the same time, I had listened to Samantha's plans for her Season, and more than half wished I could share the experience. But the first bubble had burst with Mama's marriage, and as for the second—I had to admit I knew nothing of such things beyond what I had heard in gossip at school. What did one have to do or be to qualify for a Season in London?

My mind again brought back the sneers of the girls at school and the loneliness there, and I was sure that those who were presented to the ton did not suffer such indignities. I was on the brink of womanhood, and my thoughts on it were vague and tinged with trepidation. I had been used to thinking myself a girl forever; I felt uncomfortable thinking of what came after or what would happen to me when I was a girl no longer.

Mama's marriage to Sir Jeremy was a nine days' wonder. The ton had nearly given up the thought that a hardened bachelor like Sir Jeremy would even lend his thoughts to marriage after all the eligible young ladies thrown at him year after year. The announcement of their marriage caused a sensation; who, after all, was this woman of obscure

background who had ensnared the Unsnarable?
It seemed Sir Jeremy and Mama had been extraor-
dinarily discreet; few, if any, had heard of Mrs.
Canning lately, and even the gentlemen who had
formed her admiring circle had got no nearer
than arm's length and knew only that Sir Jeremy
had been as one of them, although a little more
favored than most. Those who remembered recalled
that there were the Cannings of Somerset and
that there had been a runaway match between a
younger son and some young lady. Some others
remembered a youthful Major Canning who
bravely gave his life during the Peninsular wars
and who had left a young wife and child behind.

The curious called or left their cards. Some
claimed to have known Mama of old when Papa
had been alive; some even claimed to be related.
Of the former, Mama seemed mentally to shrug
her shoulders and accept them at their word if
they were pleasant enough. The latter fell into
three categories: the opportunists who clearly
wanted to batten on Mama's good fortune, the
Swifts, and the Cannings.

The opportunists were politely but speedily
dismissed. When it became clear what these
people were about, Mama quickly changed from
an amiable, laughing lady to an austerely mannered,
haughty matron. I was amazed at how quickly she
could make their fawning manners wilt and freeze
all conversation to a standstill.

The Swifts were entirely different. Two of Sir
Jeremy's aunts near London came to town on the
heels of the announcement. Lady Sheffield, the

eldest, was his father's sister, as was Mrs. Harris. The former, a marchioness, lived up to the dignity of the title; indeed, she made Mama quite nervous at first. Her manner was old-fashioned and austere, her countenance severe, with sharp planes and angles at cheek and chin. But she proved herself to be kindly for all that and was clearly delighted that Sir Jeremy had finally come around to do his duty to his name and produce an heir.

Mama actually blushed at this last statement; Lady Sheffield took this as a sign of great modesty in her and kindly patted her hand, saying she would do very well and that she was glad her nephew had had the sense to choose a pretty-behaved and modest young woman. This caused Mama to blush even more furiously, and she looked appealingly at Sir Jeremy; but he only grinned mischievously at her and solemnly agreed with his aunt.

Mrs. Harris was quite the opposite of Lady Sheffield; where her ladyship was all sharp angles and unbending of manner, her sister was all rounded plumpness and sighing romanticism. She had accompanied Lady Sheffield on her visit but said little beyond the exclamations of congratulation and felicity. She cast speaking glances to both her nephew and his wife, clasped her hands, sighed, and fluttered the lace of her handkerchief as she dabbed sentimentally at her eyes. After they left, I could see that Mama had become more comfortable in her new role as Lady Swift; their approval had dissipated any fears that she would not be an acceptable wife for Sir Jeremy.

It was a good thing that the Swifts had called on us before the Cannings. The Viscountess Canning deigned to cross our threshold at last, and such was her demeanor upon admittance to our parlour that an impartial bystander would have thought she had been forced to visit Newgate Prison instead of a residence at Half-Moon Street. Fortified by the knowledge that the Swifts found no fault with her—indeed approved the match—Mama was able to greet the viscountess with a calm and truly regal air.

As she was announced into our presence, Mama rose. She was looking particularly beautiful in a soft lavender-pink gown, her only ornament a single diamond pendant. The lavender color and turban on her head were the only things that distinguished her from a young girl. Her appearance was enough to give the viscountess pause as she entered the room.

She recovered, however, and came forward. "Lady Swift, I presume?" Lady Canning said haughtily.

I suppressed a frown. Who else would it be? I thought indignantly. If Mama had any similar thought, she did not reveal it. She came forward and curtsied most gracefully as her ladyship extended two wrinkled fingers. Mama barely touched them before the viscountess withdrew her hand. "I see you have done well for yourself. Sir Jeremy Swift. Very well indeed." Her hawk eyes left Mama and fixed on me. "And this . . . ?"

Mama's lips tightened, but she said coolly enough, "Georgia, your granddaughter, my lady." I gave a credible curtsy, I believe the best since

Miss Angstead's. For Mama's sake, I said to myself, I would be on my best behavior.

Lady Canning beckoned to me. "Come here, girl. I must look at you." I bridled at her arrogant voice, but after catching a warning look from Mama, I subsided and came forward. A viselike grip took hold of my chin, and I was forced to look at her ladyship. Her steel grey eyes examined me as if I were a horse, and I stared back at her lean face as calmly as I could. How rude of her, I thought to myself, even if she is my grandmother and a viscountess!

The thought must have reflected in my face, for she let go of me and emitted a short bark of laughter. "You show yourself to be a Canning, if I am not mistaken, with that look! You have your father's eyes and hair, and yes"—she flicked my chin with her finger—"that devilish stubborn chin." She turned away and glanced at Mama. "As for the rest," she said, her voice void of interest, "you take after your mother."

I grew angry again at her tone, but I lowered my eyes and said demurely, "I am so glad you think so, my lady! I have always thought Mama to be the most beautiful lady I have ever known."

I heard Mama gasp and begin to remonstrate, only to be interrupted by Lady Canning's short laugh. "Impertinent minx!" I raised my eyes and saw she had pursed her lips, but there was a glint of approval in her eyes. "You are loyal, at least."

I curtsied again. "Yes, ma'am. Mama has told me that Cannings are always so."

A "Humph!" was the response she gave to this accolade to Mama's raising of me, though she was momentarily surprised into giving Mama a sharp, assessing glance.

Mama took this break in conversation to order tea. She served it with her usual grace, and the viscountess seemed wont to take it with more of an accepting demeanor than previously.

"I have come," said her ladyship in a more expansive tone, "at an opportune time, I think." Mama looked at her questioningly. Lady Canning gave what could have been a smile. "Come now, Lady Swift, you must realize that your marriage changes things a little for you and my granddaughter."

"A little, I will admit," said Mama, smiling. "I have acquired a husband, and my daughter a father."

"More than that, I think," replied her ladyship. "You are newly married. No doubt you will be going on your honeymoon." Mama raised her eyebrows at this excursion into her private life but inclined her head. "My granddaughter is close to eighteen, if I am not mistaken, and it is time she thought of marriage, do you not agree?" Mama opened her mouth and closed it, looked at me, then nodded again. "How awkward it is, then, that you should be going on your honeymoon just as she should be having her Season, don't you think?"

Mama sank onto her chair, clearly taken aback. "It is true she is near eighteen, but Georgia is still young yet, and I had thought she would accompany us to—"

Lady Canning waved a dismissive hand. "Nothing is more awkward, I assure you, than having a young chit of a thing at one's heels during one's travels."

"Georgia would *not* be at our heels, madame!" retorted Mama with a good deal of heat, but she was cut off.

Her ladyship smiled condescendingly. "You may not think of yourself, Lady Swift, but you must think of your daughter. The sooner she enters society, the better her chances at an eligible connection. As for her youth, why, at her age I was already wed and heavy with my first child!" She gave Mama an assessing glance. "And I'll wager you were not much older, as well."

"Excuse me, my lady," I spoke up, "but I really have no thought of marriage."

"Nonsense!" exclaimed the viscountess. "I have never heard of a young lady who has not thought prodigiously about marriage." She looked at Mama as if to blame her for my unorthodox statement but saw that Mama was nodding in agreement. She sniffed but said, "And what do you think you will be doing with yourself if you do not marry?"

"I—I could become a paintrix and support myself doing portraits. Or perhaps a school-mistress," I said defiantly, but the words sounded immensely foolish in the face of her obvious scorn.

"Fiddlesticks! A more nonsensical scheme than that I have yet to hear. No, no, it's a Season you'll be wanting and a Season you'll be getting," she pronounced triumphantly.

"Excuse me, my lady"—Mama's voice was firm—"but I am not precisely sure how you may be concerned with my daughter's come-out."

The viscountess eyed her with some irony. "Loyalty, you might say. I may not have liked my son's marriage with you—and I still do not, so don't be getting any ideas—but my granddaughter is a Canning for all that, and no one can say a Canning does not make a push to do what is right. I believe I have entry into the most desirable circles; I can make sure Georgia gains entry into them, too—if, that is, I find her presentable enough."

I could see some hesitation in Mama's eyes, but she said, "I am sure that is not necessary, Lady Canning. I believe my new station is adequate enough to provide for my own daughter."

The viscountess emitted a disbelieving snort. "And whom, may I ask, do you know well enough to gain vouchers for Almack's?"

A slight flush crept up into Mama's cheeks. "No one," she whispered.

"As I thought." Her ladyship nodded with satisfaction. "You will admit that it is desirable that Georgia be married well, and that I can provide suitable entrée into the right circles." Mama nodded, glancing at me sadly. I could see she had wished to launch me into those circles herself. I said nothing, for her sake. "Then you will allow me to present my granddaughter." This was a statement that sounded very close to a command.

I looked at Mama beseechingly. I did not want to be presented by the dowager viscountess—I could hardly call her Grandmother, for she did not seem so to me. But Mama gave her head a tiny shake, saying, "I think, Georgia, your grandmother is right; it would be best for you to have an influential entrée into society. Indeed, it would be more proper that your father's family present you than Sir Jeremy's."

"But Mama! I would rather wait and have you present me. I don't care about the first circles of society. I—"

"Not care about society!" The viscountess glared at Mama. "*Your* influence, I have no doubt! No Canning would be so lost to propriety!"

"No, no! It is not Mama's fault," I cried, "it is just that I had not thought of marriage yet, I—"

"Nonsense!" stated her ladyship. "If you have not thought of marriage, it is time that you did." She turned to Mama once again. "I shall have my daughter, Lady Stoneham, call upon you. She will chaperone Georgia along with her own daughter to all the proper functions. I shall procure the vouchers for Almack's and make all the necessary introductions." She rose. "I expect my grand-daughter to be dressed in the latest mode, but in a modest manner; you may send the dressmaker's bill to me." She left before I could make any more protests.

I turned to Mama pleadingly. "Surely, Mama, you wouldn't let me go with that—that old harridan!"

"Georgia!" Mama said sharply. "You must not speak so! She is your grandmother." She did not meet my eyes, however, and was silent for a moment. She drew in a breath before saying: "It is for the best, I think. My dear, even though I am now Lady Swift, I have not the entrée to the best places where you should go to find a suitable match."

"I can wait, truly I can!" I cried.

Mama took my hands and patted them. "For how long?" She smiled sadly. "It may take more than a couple of years before I myself am established creditably, which leaves that many fewer years for you to have time to see a larger world than what I have had to offer you. If we had a wider, more respectable circle of friends, perhaps we could rely on that. But we do not; a widow like myself, you know, has to be discreet, if not entirely retiring. I want you to have more than one year to look about you for a husband." I could not look at her. "You know I mean this for the best, don't you, love?"

"Yes, Mama," I said dully. I wanted to tell her that I did not want to marry, but I knew it was useless. I felt very much alone.

Lady Stoneham called on us in less than a sennight's time. She was a somewhat vague woman but seemed willing to take me on. She assured me that I would like staying with her while Mama and Sir Jeremy were gone. Her daughter, Amelia, was an amiable girl, she said, and she was sure we would become firm friends. I did not think much of her, but I doubt I would have thought much of anyone who would come from the dowager viscountess.

Both Mama and I packed at the same time, she for her honeymoon, I for Lady Stoneham's house. We did not speak to each other much the week before our departure; indeed, we spoke less than usual with each other after Lady Canning's visit. I was not inclined to talk. I wandered about our house, even

passing through the servants' quarters. I would
not live in this house again. Mama's solicitor was
selling it while she was on her honeymoon and I
at Lady Stoneham's. When Mama came back she
would live with Sir Jeremy—and I as well, if I did
not "take" in my first Season.

I felt awhirl with uncertainty and fear; I was
abruptly presented with a London Season, and
while I had wistfully thought of the possibility, I
had not seen it as a reality or that it would come
upon me so soon. Then there was the frightening
prospect of being presented not by someone I
knew and loved, but by complete strangers, for all
they were my family.

And what came after my Season? What if I did
not do well? What came after that? I did not care to
think about it, but the questions persisted, and it
seemed I retired to bed more often than not with
the headache. Mama cast me a few anxious looks
all the while, but I merely smiled at her. I did not
want to let her know my trepidation; indeed, I hardly
knew how to voice my fears, so uncertain was I.

My smiles must have reassured her, for when
she was not looking concerned, she was smiling
dreamily, absently playing with various trinkets
she had packed in her bandboxes and leaving
them out on her bed. Grimley merely sighed and
put them back in. Mama's dreaminess depressed
me further, even though I had intended for all
this to happen—her marriage and my push for
independence. Perversely, the more I smiled and
reassured her, the more I wished I did not feel as
though all the world were abandoning me.

Mama went with me one afternoon to Lady Stoneham's town house in Pall Mall, to see me settled in. I had expected a dark and gloomy interior and was further depressed to find the house as light and airy as ours. Lady Stoneham was all vague assurances that I would fit in well and would find all to my comfort.

This seemed to reassure Mama, and she kissed me farewell. She threw off her newlywed haze for a moment to look at me solemnly. "We never did talk about your injury and what happened when you came home with Lord Ashcombe, did we, love?" She touched my cheek gently. "I think I shall not say more than this: I believe you may trust Lord Ashcombe. He is a good young man."

"Still setting your cap for me, are you, Mama?"

"He cares for you, I think," said Mama. She looked at me as if to ask if I cared for him in return, but she did not speak.

"But then, we have not seen him this age, have we not?" I replied lightly.

Mama merely shook her head at me. She touched my cheek again, then gave me a hug. I shall not cry, I told myself sternly, and smiled, kissing her in return.

She finally left. I looked about the drawing room and then silently down at my hands. A small plump one covered mine and patted them. "So brave of you not to cry, my dear," murmured Lady Stoneham. I looked up. Lady Stoneham smiled kindly. "I know I would have. Perhaps you would like to rest for a while; I shall show you your room myself. Then when you are rested, you shall meet

Amelia; she is out with a friend, but she should be back in an hour." She rose. "Do let's go up, shall we?"

I followed her upstairs and was shown to a pretty pink-and-white room. I felt a little better. Lady Stoneham seemed quite kind. Perhaps it was not going to be so bad after all. She left after fluffing the pillows on the bed, and I lay down for a while. I suppose I was more tired than I thought, for when I next opened my eyes, the sun had sunk considerably, and I judged it close to dinner-time. I sprang up and rang for a maid to help me prepare for it.

I dressed in good time and descended the stairs. Lady Stoneham glanced up and upon seeing me smiled and beckoned. "Ah, just in time, I see! Amelia is here, and her friend, too. I am sure you shall be bosom bows in no time at all," she prophesied. Lady Stoneham ushered me into the parlour. "Amelia!" she cried, "do see who is here! Georgia, I would like you to meet my daughter, Amelia. Amelia, this is Georgia Canning."

I curtsied and held out my hand. Amelia was a pleasant enough looking girl, a bit on the plump side, blue eyes as vague as her mother's, and softly waving brown hair. She smiled. "Pleased to meet you," she murmured politely. Her eyes met mine, then wandered away. She may have been pleased, but she did not seem interested. I shrugged mentally. She seemed agreeable enough; we should rub along tolerably well, I thought.

"And this," said Lady Stoneham, turning from Amelia to the girl behind her, "is Amelia's dear friend, Lady Caroline Emmett-Johns."

I turned swiftly to see if my ears had deceived me. I discovered they had not. It was indeed Caroline Emmett-Johns, looking as if butter wouldn't melt in her mouth. Of all the people I had to meet now, it had to be her.

9

I knew Caroline from Miss Angstead's Seminary for Young Ladies, and I detested her. She was
the reason Mama decided to ask that I be a parlour
boarder at Miss Angstead's, for Caroline had tor-
mented me endlessly there. Perhaps Caroline did it
at first because I was different from the others.
Perhaps also it was because I never could toady to
her, which she expected from everyone who
entered her sphere of influence. She may have
been an earl's daughter, but I never could curl my
tongue around a compliment just to flatter.

I suppose if I had just suffered in silence, she
would have contented herself with mere contempt. But I think she became my only true enemy
because of the frog. Truly, it wasn't *my* fault,
because *I* didn't put it under her pillow. I wouldn't

have touched the nasty thing, for I hated frogs. It was Mama, really. Once, when Mama visited me at Miss Angstead's, she laid her hand by my pillow and, after a startled jump, pulled something out from under it.

There, in front of my eyes, was a frog, dangling by a hind leg held daintily between my mother's index finger and thumb. Its bulbous eyes blinked solemnly at me. I shrank back.

"Ugh! Please put it away," I said, shivering with disgust.

"Mmmm. I did not think you usually kept such things in your bed," she replied calmly. "Who put it there?"

I had no proof, so I did not want to say, but I could not help looking down the room toward a certain bed.

Mama rose to put the frog out the window, then paused. She smiled a wide and slightly wicked smile and slid the loathsome creature under a pillow two beds down. It was Caroline Emmett-Johns's.

It was on that day that Mama had decided I would become a parlour boarder. It was satisfying to see the other girls' envious faces when I went to my new room and even more gratifying when I heard Caroline Emmett-Johns's shriek of disgust later that night. I knew afterward that she must have made one of her sycophants put the frog in my bed. Whenever she had the chance (which was seldom, once I had become a parlour boarder, thank goodness!), she played tricks on me, and they were more mean-spirited than ever before.

And who else would have known where the frog had originally been placed?

And now, as I went forward to greet Caroline as politely as I could, I looked in her eyes and knew she had forgotten nothing. Her lips lifted in a small smile, but her eyes were just as assessing, just as cold, as they were when she was at Miss Angstead's.

Caroline rose and curtsied and held out her hand. I raised mine as well, but she barely touched my fingers before she drew away. "I believe we have met," I said boldly. I was proud to find my voice did not waver.

"Yes," said Caroline. "I believe we have." She tried to sound pleased.

Lady Stoneham nodded. "There! I knew it. You shall all rub along very well; you are acquainted after all. How delightful!" This last remark seemed to be directed at the door; the butler entered and announced dinner.

We removed ourselves to the dining room, and Lady Stoneham waved us to our chairs. I stared at Caroline, wondering if she had changed much since I had last seen her. She picked up a napkin as a cup of tea was placed in front of her. Caroline smiled at me and said lightly, "Having tea is so civilized, don't you think? And what a blessing napkins are, too! I wonder what our ancestors did when they dirtied their hands before tea?" She looked at me meaningfully as she deliberately scrubbed her right hand on the tablecloth. "You must know, Miss Canning; you were the scholarly one at school, I remember." I heard a sycophantic giggle from Amelia. Lady Stoneham smiled vaguely but pleasantly.

Lady Stoneham, I thought grimly, should never take up soothsaying. It seemed Caroline Emmett-Johns had not changed at all.

I almost felt as if I were back at Miss Angstead's. I had to bear the snubs of Caroline Emmett-Johns again, and if there was not a fawning group of girls around her, as there was at the Seminary, Amelia did a fine job of making up for the lack of numbers. There was not a day spent in her company that did not consist of "Lady Caroline said," or "Lady Caroline heard," or "Lady Caroline went to," until I was near to screaming with vexation. I suppose Amelia would have been an amiable enough girl, but she had not a thought in her head other than what Caroline might have put there.

Caroline was a frequent caller at the Stonehams', and Lady Stoneham approved the acquaintance since Caroline was from one of the first families and so amiable, too—to her uncritical eyes. I will say one thing for Caroline: she was nothing if not subtle. She said nothing that was not unexceptional on the face of it; her gestures, the tone of her voice, and her glances, however, conveyed her meaning well enough. Only two things seemed beyond her sneers: those clearly superior to her in rank and consequence, and the male of the species.

I discovered this when Samantha came to call

one day so that we could decide on some ribbons for our hair. I was in the parlour trying to keep my expression as bland and uninterested as possible; it was not easy with Amelia and Caroline giggling rudely across from me. I rose with real delight and relief when the butler announced, "Miss Samantha Ashcombe!"

"Samantha!" I cried. "How good of you to call on me!"

She smiled but held up her hand. "Not for long, however. I only called to see if you wanted to come with me to the draper's. I need to see if there are any ribbons that match my new dress." She looked past me at Amelia and nodded her acknowledgment, then glanced questioningly at Caroline.

I recalled myself then and introduced them. "Are you, by any chance, ah, related to Lord Ashcombe?" asked Caroline.

Samantha inclined her head. "Yes, he is my brother."

Caroline glanced briefly at me. A speculative look grew in her eye. "How enjoyable it would be to drive to a shop on a lovely day like this!" she exclaimed wistfully.

"Alas, if I had known Georgia had company, I would have called for a larger carriage. But there is only room for perhaps one more, and that would be a tight squeeze indeed." Samantha's kind smile encompassed us all.

"Oh, well, Amelia need not come," Caroline began; she did not notice how her friend's face fell, but she was stopped by Samantha's shocked gaze. "What I mean is, I daresay Amelia would not want to come along; indeed, she was just saying she was feeling the migraine before you entered."

I lifted my eyebrows as I surveyed Amelia's pink cheeks and bright eyes. "How odd," I said ironically. "I do not recall Amelia saying anything of the sort; she certainly does not look sickly."

Caroline laughed lightly, "Ah, Miss Ashcombe, you must know that dear Georgia is of a studious inclination; your academic, whose mind is attuned to loftier thoughts, cannot help but pass over the more mundane aspects of life."

Samantha looked at me in surprise, then back at Caroline. "There may be some people who are like that. I have not noticed it in Georgia, nor in such a studious person as my brother. Indeed, it was my brother's perception which saw fit to introduce me to Georgia, and he was quite right in supposing we would get along quite famously."

Caroline's mouth fell open at this point, but she shut it swiftly. I smiled sweetly at her. It was obvious she had not thought I had yet met Lucas, and it was even farther from her mind that I should have met him before I met Samantha.

"Well, I cannot keep the horses waiting," Samantha said briskly. "Perhaps, since Miss Stoneham has the migraine, we can postpone our outing for another time. For now, I hope you can do without Georgia; we shall not be gone long." She waved her hand at me. "Do fetch your pelisse, Georgia, and we shall go. I shall be waiting in the carriage." She gave a polite but businesslike nod to Caroline and Amelia as I left the room.

As I entered the carriage, Samantha gave me a questioning glance. "I do not want to offend you if she is your friend, Georgia, but I hope you don't know anyone else so—so pushing! It makes one positively uncomfortable."

"You needn't have any compunction about it, I assure you. I knew her at Miss Angstead's, but she is a friend of Amelia's, not mine, thank Heaven!" I paused thoughtfully. "It's odd, but Caroline is usually a bit more subtle than that."

"How so?"

"Oh, she's quite good at—" I stopped, not wanting to seem cattish.

"At—?" prompted Samantha.

"Oh, nothing, really. She, ah, usually has a more polite manner than what she displayed just now. I'm not sure what came over her."

"You are withholding something from me." Samantha looked at me keenly.

"It's just that I'm probably being a cat and taking what she says too seriously. There's nothing in anything she says, to be sure."

"But quite a lot in what she doesn't say, if I am not mistaken."

"Yes!" I cried, and released from my constraint by her observation, I confided my distrust of Caroline.

After a while, Samantha nodded. "I don't think you're mistaken about her attitude; after all, Lucas and I say all sorts of blunt things to you and you've never seemed to take anything we say personally! Even when you should!"

I laughed. "No, that's because you are my friends!"

"Humph!" Samantha said mock huffily. "At any rate, she seems just the sort who would make remarks like that." She paused. "How much would you wager that she will be treating you with more respect from now on?"

I blinked at this unexpected observation. "I don't know what you mean. Why should she treat me any differently from before? Because I happen to know you?"

"No, because you know Lucas," she replied bluntly. I looked at her, puzzled. "Caroline reminds me of an acquaintance of Mama's: Mrs. Bennington. All coos and sweet murmurings, and quite pretty, but a terrible flirt. She had no compunction whatsoever about gaining introductions through her lady friends so that she could cut them out with the men they knew. And one never could seem to fault her, for she never was outwardly unpleasant about it."

"Well, I think Caroline could be quite unpleasant about it."

"Caroline is just not practiced enough, that is all," replied Samantha.

I pondered this. "So you are saying that just because I know Lucas, she will be kind to me so that she might gain an introduction to him?"

Samantha nodded.

I didn't know what to think of this. I shrugged. "Well, we'll see what comes of it," I said complacently as we stepped down from the carriage into the draper's.

Samantha was quite right. Caroline had gone by the time I came back, but the next time she visited, she was all solicitude and kindness. I smiled at her but was wary; I would think about this and see what I could make of it.

10

The Season began.

There is nothing like London, I think, when the Season begins. Before it, there are the people who usually live in the City all of the time: the merchants, the fruit and bread sellers, and the like. There are those, like Mama and myself, who live year round in a rented or owned town house. There are those landed gentry who find country life far too dull and boring for their exalted palates and who only set foot on their estates on repairing leases; there are fewer of those in these more enlightened days, when a landlord at least knows that his pleasures can be funded only if his estates and people are well kept.

London seems sparse and lean and grey in the winter, like a poor old woman I once saw in Tothill on my way back from school. Yet, it is wrong when people say cities have no season; when spring comes, London throws off her foggy grey shroud. Brass fixtures gleam on wooden doors, while ladies in their flower-petal dresses and gentlemen in their wasp-waist coats flit from door to door like so many bees in a field.

Before Lady Stoneham, Amelia, and I could do our share of flitting, however, we had to have ourselves done over in the latest fashion. If I said that my dress fitting for Samantha's party was a trial, I now withdraw the statement. That, compared with the millions of fittings I had to endure for my new wardrobe, was a romp in the park. I do not know how many times I was stitched in and out, pinned and unpinned, and made to turn around and around until I was dizzy. We made countless trips to the Pantheon Bazaar for this frippery or that, at bargain prices we simply could not resist.

It was done, finally—the foundation wardrobe, that is. When I breathed a sigh of relief and remarked that I was glad our wardrobes were complete, Lady Stoneham looked at me in surprise. "No, no, my dear! You quite mistake the matter! What we have now is quite enough to start with, but we can hardly be seen at all the balls we are going to wearing the same dress twice! *That* would be deadly. After we put in appearances at a few places, we shall see what the lay of the land is, so to speak, and modify our wardrobes accordingly."

I bowed my head to her dictum, for I knew it

would please Mama for me to be presented at my best, and this was apparently the best. I would not bow my head to be shorn, however; I looked with horror at the latest Titus coiffure in *La Belle Assemblée*. My hair, though not the guinea gold of Mama's or the fashionable black of Samantha's, was my best feature; I enjoyed having its thick chestnut waves loose and cozy around me when I was by myself. I would be fitted and pinned to Lady Stoneham's heart's content, but I would not be shorn like a sheep. I made that unfortunate remark in front of Caroline, and she could not resist saying, "No, you are right, Georgia; you would hardly want to look like a sheep," smiling as if to say that I looked like one now.

That almost made me want to cut my hair right then and there, but Lady Stoneham forestalled me by giving me a keen glance and saying: "No, I cannot see you with a crop, Georgia. We shall see for certain when you don the white sarcenet ball gown with mint-green trim. There shall be time enough then to crop it if need be."

The time came when I did wear the white sarcenet ball gown. It was quite lovely, though while I now saw that a décolletage was the usual style, I was still not used to the puffed sleeves just off the shoulders or the way I seemed to be more well endowed than I should have been when I wore it.

Lady Stoneham nodded when she saw me in it. "No, we will not cut your hair. You shall have it styled in a chignon; the dress has classic lines, and we will continue the theme in your coiffure."

She had the maid put up my hair, and I stared at myself in the mirror. The lady with burnished hair, deep green eyes, and long white column of neck and smooth shoulders did not seem at all to be me.

I had thought Lady Stoneham a scatterbrain, but where fashion was concerned, there was nothing she did not know and nothing that escaped her notice. Proof of that were the approving glances I received from both respectable matrons and young gentlemen alike when she took us to the Countess of Gresham's ball for her daughter, Lady Diana. It seemed I was neither dressed beyond what was proper nor behindhand on *à la modalité*. I felt anxious at the ball, for it was my first real one and very large.

I nervously touched the pearl necklace that Mama had given me for my birthday before she left and felt a little reassured. It was as if I could feel a bit of Mama's presence around me, and it reminded me that I was no longer seventeen but just turned eighteen—a lady now, and I must act like one.

Lady Stoneham was attending to Amelia, who was by turns excited and overcome by shyness. I did not know quite what to do myself. I sat wondering what I would say if someone asked me to dance. Something shy and demure? Witty? Sophisticated? I unfurled my fan and fanned myself as I supposed an experienced ball frequenter would, but it was a mistake; I had brought the fan that Lucas had given me, and it reminded me of what happened after Samantha's party. I did not

want to think of it—it made me more nervous
than ever. I shut it.

"Georgia!"

I turned on my chair—Samantha to the rescue!
I breathed a sigh of relief. Here at last was someone I knew and could talk with in case I did not
know what else to do. She was truly beautiful in a
shimmering pale blue satin gown with a net
overdress; my heart swelled with pride that I had
such a friend. Behind her was Lady Ashcombe,
who nodded to me briefly before she turned back
to the lady with whom she was talking.

"I am so glad to see you here! I could hug you!"
she exclaimed, then dropped her hands and took
on a mock serious mien. "But no. We are sophisticated ladies, and ladies do not hug, do they? Ah,
yes!" She bent forward and gingerly took me by
the shoulders, brushing her cheek lightly with
mine. "There! Now that we have thrown a bone to
propriety, we can get on as we please!"

We both laughed, causing a few heads to turn
in our direction. I caught the eye of a gentleman
and looked away shyly, but not before he smiled
at me. We quieted immediately, for we also had
caught looks from some old-fashioned-looking
dowagers.

"Georgia! Miss Ashcombe!" We both turned at
Lady Stoneham's voice. She bustled up, and in her
wake was the gentleman who had smiled at me
earlier. He was not a tall man, but of a good
height, with light brown hair and a pair of broad
shoulders that amply filled out his coat. I felt shy
but managed to smile at him as Lady Stoneham

introduced Mr. Landsbury to us. He bowed to me and smiled back, then turned to Samantha. A warm and admiring look grew in his eyes as he gazed at her, and I knew Samantha had made a conquest. Lady Stoneham left us to attend to another young man who seemed desirous of meeting Amelia.

"I confess," Mr. Landsbury said ruefully, "I do not know which one of you lovely young ladies to ask for a dance first."

"Oh, you must ask Samantha first," I blurted. "She is much prettier than I am!" I blushed at my precipitousness.

Samantha's color rose, but a dimple appeared in her cheek. "Oh, but you must ask Georgia first, for she is a far better dancer than I am." She cast me a challenging grin.

Mr. Landsbury laughed. "Confronted by Grace and Beauty both! But that is a harder decision than ever!"

"Well, I suppose you must properly select by rank, then; so it must be Samantha," I said primly. That should do it, I thought.

"Age before beauty," Samantha retorted triumphantly.

"Why—!" I shut my mouth, then burst out laughing. Mr. Landsbury grinned and held out his arm to me. "Only wait until I return, Samantha!" I shook my finger threateningly at her as I put a hand on my partner's arm.

"Behold me shaking in my slippers," drawled Samantha, casting Mr. Landsbury a mischievous look from under her lashes. His look of admiration grew.

It was an enjoyable dance, but I sensed Mr. Landsbury was quite preoccupied. I did not mind, however; I was sure it was because of Samantha. The dance soon ended, and I felt easier as he escorted me back to where Samantha was sitting. I felt I had acquitted myself well on the dance floor, with little need to worry I would do otherwise. As we stopped next to Samantha, I saw Mr. Landsbury's face brighten. I lifted an eyebrow at my friend and grinned. She blushed a little as she went off with him.

I did not lack for partners after that; Lady Stoneham was like a hen with wayward chicks in the way she was fluttering back and forth between Amelia and myself, introducing respectable young men to us. Amelia, somewhat to my surprise, had a small crowd about her; but on reflection, she did seem less objectionable whenever Caroline was not about.

It was in the middle of a quadrille, I think, when I looked up past my partner's shoulder and almost stumbled. I apologized hastily, and when the dance was over, I hurried as decorously as I could to Samantha, who had just been released by her partner amid fulsome compliments. I waited until she sent him to procure some lemonade.

"Samantha! You did not tell me your brother was in town again!" I whispered fiercely.

"No! Is he?" she exclaimed. "I did not know! Where did you see him?"

There was no need for me to point him out: Lucas was threading his way through the crowd toward us. A small tremor went through me at the sight of his tall figure. I looked away, hoping he did not see me. Silly of me, since he *was* coming toward us. But I did *not* seem to be able to think very coherently at that point.

"Lucas!" cried Samantha, and seemed about to throw herself upon her brother's impeccable cravat. He deftly caught her hands before she could do so.

"Good Lord, Samantha, I've never seen one so inclined to maul a person about as you! And at a ball, of all places!" He shook his head. "And yes, I know. You *are* glad to see me, and when did I get into town!"

She giggled. "Yes, and you can let go of my hands, you odious creature! I promise not to rumple your neckcloth, truly. But stay! You are totally ignoring Georgia; she is here at the ball, too!"

I could not hide behind Samantha; Lucas looked above her head at me, and I came out from behind. "I am happy to see you again," I said. He took my hand and bowed over it, very elegantly.

He smiled and his eyes grew warm, just as Mr. Landsbury's did when he looked at Samantha. "I think I can hardly ignore her, Sam. May I reserve the next dance, Miss Georgia?" he said gallantly.

I blushed and stammered, "I—I don't know. That is, the next one is a waltz, and I think I need to have Lady Stoneham's permission before I can." I *had* been approved to dance the waltz at Almack's already, but I was unsure if it was only there I could waltz or if that approval extended elsewhere as well.

"We shall see," he returned, and promptly left

my side. I felt bewildered at his sudden departure and looked at Samantha questioningly. She only gazed at me with what seemed to be a laugh in her eyes. Lucas returned with Lady Stoneham.

"Of course you may dance the waltz, silly girl!" Lady Stoneham smiled at me. "Once you have been approved to dance it at Almack's, you may dance it anywhere. Now, no more missishness, and do enjoy your dance with Lord Ashcombe." She waved a hand at us and bustled away.

Lucas took my hand and led me out to the floor. As his hand went about my waist, I shivered but managed to get my wits about me; this was nothing more than a dance, after all. I felt shy all of a sudden and could not look at him above his neckcloth. "Yes, I do think I tied it quite well, if I say so myself," said Lucas after a while.

I looked up at him. "I'm sorry if I have not much conversation right now."

His brows raised, but he smiled and said, "And I am sorry I did not have a chance to see how you were recuperating before I left. I am glad to see you well."

My eyes fell. "Yes," I said tonelessly.

His voice softened. "Did you mind so much?"

I felt confused and a little panicky. I attempted a laugh. "To be sure, it was not all that pleasant to be ill, but as you see, I am fully recovered. And— and I have got the fan you sent me; I have brought it, you see."

"Glad you like it." His voice sounded withdrawn; I looked in his eyes, and they seemed cooler than before.

"Indeed I do!" I chattered on. "I have not seen anything like it, and so beautifully painted, too!"

He murmured something appropriate, and I chattered on like a skitter wit. I felt like a fool. It was with a feeling of relief that I left the dance floor. It made the situation no better to discover, as he brought me back to Lady Stoneham, that Caroline Emmett-Johns was talking with Amelia next to her. Her eyes flickered here and there around the ballroom until she saw Lucas beside me. Unless I wanted to be horridly rude, I had no choice but to introduce them.

"I am pleased to meet you, Lord Ashcombe," said Caroline after I made the introduction. She looked at him demurely from beneath her eyelashes and smiled dulcetly. He grinned in his engaging way, and I felt curiously bereft. I did not deceive myself. Caroline was a very pretty girl, tall and slender, with her honey-blond curls and light blue eyes. Her jonquil gown with the gauze overdress was cut close to her form, and the décolletage and tiny puffed sleeves revealed a good expanse of creamy whiteness. How could he not admire her? My thoughts were confirmed as he asked her for the next dance, and she threw me a triumphant glance as he led her to the dance floor.

I put on my most brilliant smile, determined not to let the sight of Caroline dancing indecently close to Lucas ruin my enjoyment of the ball. I transferred my gaze to a young man just to the side of the couple, gave him a scintillating smile, and mentally willed him to offer me a dance. This he seemed to do quite willingly, and I continued to dance my way through the rest of the night, as others claimed me for a dance as well.

If I was not bubbling with exclamations of pleasure when we departed, I think I expressed a suitable amount of appreciation. Somehow, I did not care to let Lady Stoneham or Amelia know that I was retiring with a raging headache.

Samantha had been right. Caroline's demeanor went through a change overnight. Now that I was no longer useful to her, now that she had received an introduction to Lucas, she no longer had a need to be so kind.

Not that it mattered to me, I said to myself. After the Greshams' ball, I was surprised to find that some of my dance partners came to call on me. I did not know why they should, for after the last dance I had with Lucas, I did nothing but chatter what I thought were inanities. I smiled to myself while my callers and I exchanged commonplaces. I wondered how quickly they would leave if I dared discuss Mrs. Wollstonecraft's essays with them. Of course I did not, for Lady Stoneham had been kind to me, and I did not want to scandalize her.

But then, Caroline's demeanor did begin to matter. First there were the schoolgirl pranks—brambles in one's bed, being short-sheeted, et cetera. I had experienced them before when I had been a new student at Miss Angstead's, and it was easy to tell where the inspiration for these tricks came from. Caroline's eager looks when she visited and the whispers between her and Amelia were evidence enough for me. I had a difficult time not being ill at the sight of Caroline's falsely smiling face whenever others were around.

Indeed, I had a difficult time not being ill at the sight of Lucas squiring her around. For an intelligent man, he was singularly blind to her true nature, I thought. She had only to smile at him from a distance and he would cross the room to her. I noticed that other men would as well, but they had the excuse of not being all that intelligent, so it was easy to see how they would succumb to her stratagems.

I thought at first to relate my encounters with Caroline to Mama in a letter. But I did not. I wrote frequently, mostly for my own amusement, for Mama and Sir Jeremy were in Vienna, and it took a long time for letters to travel that far. I did not want to worry her; she deserved her happiness, and I was surely old enough to control my own life. So my letters were filled only with gossip, what I wore, and what I did at balls and routs.

I still did see Lucas when I went out with Samantha, but although he was friendly enough, he kept his distance. I, meanwhile, was polite. Samantha noticed this, for during a ride in Hyde Park, she laid a hand on my arm and said tentatively, "I do not mean to pry, Georgia, but, well, you do still like Lucas, do you not?"

I laughed and said in a brittle voice, "Why, of

course. I can hardly dislike a brother of yours, Samantha. That would make things quite uncomfortable between you and me, and I would not want that."

She gazed at me seriously. "That is not quite what I mean. I mean, well, are you *fond* of him?"

I was not sure how to answer her. "Fond" was not the word for it. And I knew at this moment I felt vulnerable—Samantha was his sister, after all. How much of our conversation reached his ears each day? I did not know. And how could I let any idea of my feelings for him reach him when I knew him to be besotted with Caroline? I pinned on a smile. "Fond . . . well, I would not put it that way. Certainly I would call him a friend. Somewhat the way you are my friend, Samantha." There. I had not lied, nor had I revealed my true feelings.

Samantha seemed to ponder this. "He is very fond of you, Georgia. More, I think, than as a friend."

My heart beat a little faster, but I remembered Caroline waltzing in his arms with effortless grace at the last ball, so I shrugged carelessly and said, "*I* would not know it, and I am sure you are mistaken. Why, you only need eyes in your head to see how taken up he is with Caroline Emmett-Johns! She has gone with him in his phaeton dozens of times; she told me so herself!"

"Once, actually," replied Samantha with a small smile. "Hardly dozens."

"And of course, he never fails to dance twice with her," I continued relentlessly. "She is tall and quite lovely; it is not surprising that *any* man would want to dance attendance on her."

"But so are you beautiful!" exclaimed my friend.

I smiled at her and patted her hand. "You are very kind, Samantha. But my figure is only good, my hair is not and never shall be a fashionable color, and as for my face—while Sir Jeremy once said I was getting to look somewhat like Mama—I know I shall never achieve her looks."

Samantha shook her head, smiling. "If you persist in having a fit of the dismals, I suppose I cannot convince you. Perhaps Lucas—"

"Don't you dare—!" I gasped.

"Maybe I will, maybe I won't!" she said mischievously. She turned a deaf ear to my remonstrances.

I could not tell if Samantha had listened to me or not, for though Lucas paid me a little more attention, his attentions to Caroline also seemed to grow greater. Proportionally, I seemed to be shunned more and more by Caroline and Amelia. Not that I cared, I told myself. Not, that is, until the accidents began to happen.

It was on the night of Lady Amberley's ball for her daughter Sophia that the maid who attended both Amelia and myself gave a loud shriek as she pulled my mint-green dress from my wardrobe. "Oh, miss!" she cried, pointing a trembling finger at the dress she had laid on my bed. "Oh, miss!"

I approached it cautiously, in case there might have been a spider on it. I saw nothing of the sort and raised an eyebrow at her. "What is it, Annie? I don't see anything."

"It's ruined! Oh, miss, I swear I didn't do it! It was perfect when I last took it out! Oh, lawks, miss! Please don't have me turned away!" She started sobbing hysterically.

"Now, Annie, get hold of yourself!" I shook her shoulders gently and made her sit down. "No one is going to turn you away. Only tell me what is wrong."

She ran a trembling hand over the dress and pulled it forward. She did not have to point it out: just to the left of center, there was a tremendous slash in it that split it from bodice to hem. For a few moments I could only blink in shock. I drew in a breath. "Oh, heavens!" I whispered to myself. I could not imagine anyone committing such a wanton act of destruction. "Annie, how could this happen?"

"I don't know, miss!" the maid cried, weeping. "Please, what will you tell the mistress? I couldn't have done such a thing—'twas my favorite of your dresses, miss, like a princess's! Oh, please don't say I did it, for I swear I did not!"

"Hush, now!" I commanded. "I won't tell Lady Stoneham anything but that it was my fault, that— that it was a bit small, and it split when I put it on."

Annie shook her head dolefully. "She'll never believe you, miss. It's not that sort of tear."

"Well, then, I'll tell her I was clumsy and it ripped when I stepped on it." I patted her on her thin shoulders. "Whatever I say, you shall not be at fault, I assure you."

"But what will you wear to Lady Amberley's?"

I stopped. There was nothing I had not worn already to a ball; the new dresses I was to have for the next ones were due tomorrow. The only thing I could think of was to cry off from this one, saying I had the headache. Only . . . Perhaps this was precisely what the mysterious vandal wanted me to do. I sat up decisively. "Annie, please fetch her ladyship to me. I want to show her this. And—stop wailing now, do!—I promise I'll say it was my fault."

A moment later Lady Stoneham bustled in, a worried frown in place of her usual placid vagueness. "My dear Georgia, Annie is so upset, I cannot make heads or tails of what she is saying!"

"It's this dress, ma'am. I'm afraid I was terribly clumsy, and it ripped right through to the hem!" I hung my head, guilt personified. "I well deserve missing Lady Amberley's ball, I know, but the floors have just been waxed, and I'm afraid the rug slipped out from under me. Indeed, my new dresses have not arrived, so unless I wear something I have worn before, I do not see how I can attend."

Lady Stoneham spread the skirt of the dress and gasped in horror. "Oh, my dear girl! You say you slipped, but I cannot see—! Oh, dear! This beautiful dress!" She threw up her hands, then started to wring them. "It is too late to ask for your new dresses from Miss Strachey's. I shall have to agree that you shall have to—

"But stay! I think I may have it!" Her eyes had suddenly lost their usual vagueness and grew sharp and assessing. She pushed Annie out the door. "Go and fetch my sewing basket, swiftly, girl!" She turned to my wardrobe and started pushing aside one dress after another. "Ah, here it is!" She pulled out a white petticoat and laid it next to the dress. Annie appeared, puffing, with my lady's workbasket. Quickly Lady Stoneham seized a pair of scissors and cut another slash to the right of center, identical to the one on the left. She then clipped off the ruffles that lined both neck and hem.

"Oh, my lady!" Annie wailed.

"Hush, girl!" commanded Lady Stoneham. "This may be the greatest inspiration I have had yet!" She searched in her workbasket and brought out a roll of pale yellow ribbon, worked in silver thread, and laid it next to the slashes on the dress. "Perfect," she murmured. Swiftly she cut five pieces from the roll and stitched the ribbon to one edge of the cut dress. After some initial confusion, Annie swiftly followed suit and started stitching ribbons to the skirt and just under the bodice where the slashes began. It seemed but a few minutes before Lady Stoneham sat back and beckoned to me. "Put it on, my dear. Let us see if I have not totally ruined it."

I put on the petticoat and slipped on the dress. The petticoat was fuller than I would have worn with this particular dress, and it caused the split skirt to widen more than it had in the beginning. I looked in the mirror and saw that it almost gave the effect of an overdress, except that there were two splits instead of one, which caused the front panel of green fabric to drape in an apronlike way.

Taking the ruffles from the neck and hem deepened the décolletage and lengthened the line from bosom to foot. It looked austerely Grecian with the wide swath of embroidered ribbon lining the edges and gave me an air of elegant sophistication.

"Oh, Lady Stoneham!" I breathed in awe. "It is even better than it was before!" Impulsively I hugged her. "You are a genius!"

She put me from her but smiled, pleased. "I am hardly that, but I will admit I do have a sense of style." She beamed benevolently. "I cannot do this all the time, however, for it exhausts me. So you must give me your word you will not ruin any more dresses, young lady!" I hastened to assure her I would not. She rose and glanced at the mantelpiece clock. "Goodness! It lacks but half an hour until we must be at Lady Amberley's! We shall be late, but not terribly. I must see to Amelia. Such a slow child sometimes!" She hurried out with Annie in her train.

An undermaid who had some ability at hairdressing was called to assist me, and my hair was brought up in a Grecian knot to match my dress. A single pendant necklace was fastened around my neck and a thin chain of a bracelet about my wrist. Simplicity was the theme tonight.

I descended the stairs to the parlour, where Lady Stoneham and Amelia were waiting for me. At my entrance, her ladyship nodded approvingly at me, but to my astonishment Amelia gave me one surprised and frightened glance, then looked down at her feet, blushing furiously. I knew immediately that she had had something to do with the slashing of my dress. When she looked up again, I managed a sweet smile. That would teach her.

If Amelia was the only problem, I would have gone on as I had until Mama came back for me. But there was Caroline as well to deal with. The ball at Lady Amberley's was quite a crush, and I was gratified to find that Lady Stoneham did indeed have a genius for fashion, for I had more compliments on my dress and requests for the direction of my dressmaker than ever before. It was apparent, too, that Caroline did not expect my appearance at the ball, for she was clearly startled when she saw me and glanced angrily at Amelia. I merely smiled. I gave her another especially sweet smile when Lucas came up to ask me for a dance.

I was less nervous than I had been before with Lucas—most likely because I was still angry about my dress, and he seemed more attentive than he had lately been. I tried not to think of what had gone on before between us, but as we danced around the ballroom, I could not help but think again of that carriage ride. I managed to smile at him, and it seemed a warmth came back in his eyes, and it was almost as if the old Lucas I had known had come back.

"You look beautiful, you know," Lucas said abruptly after a brief conversational foray into last week's weather.

"Oh, practicing our social flirting, are we?" I said. I felt my face heat suddenly, and my heart beat faster than our dance warranted.

Lucas grinned. "No, I think you know well

enough how to do that. Besides, I am not really one for flirting."

"No?" I said. "Then you pretend to do so quite well with that piece of flummery you just uttered."

"Not flummery at all. We are friends, after all—no need to stand on ceremony with each other. You look beautiful."

I laughed a little shakily. Friends. I felt comforted by this, but strangely wistful. "Really, how can you say so? You were in love with my mother, after all; you must know I shall never achieve her looks!" I could not look at him, and my gaze lowered to his neckcloth.

An exasperated sigh burst above my head and made me look up at him. "*Must* you bring that up?" said Lucas, looking harassed. "I really would rather forget that. It was a mistake, and I own I was foolish to be so infatuated."

"Well, there! You see?" I returned. "You could not help it—and you have not been the only one so taken with Mama—because she *is* truly beautiful. *You* could not stop yourself any more than a bee could help stopping at a nectar-filled flower, and neither can any other man." I sighed. "I shall never have that happen to me, I think."

"Just as well if it doesn't," Lucas said cryptically.

I raised my brows at him, but he did not respond, for the dance ended, and we stopped not far from Caroline. He made me promise to give him another dance, and for Caroline's benefit, I smiled brightly and agreed. I wanted to ask Lucas about his last comment, but his attention was claimed by a white-haired dowager who said she once knew his grandmother. He looked apologetically at me before he bent his attention to the lady.

I glanced at Caroline. She had a fair-haired man by her side, and I assumed she would ignore me, for she had little time for females when there was a man about. But she turned to me and smiled. "My dear Miss Canning, I would dearly love to introduce you to Sir Harlow Smythe. He has been desiring a dance with you this age, and here you are!"

Sir Harlow smiled at me. He was not nearly as handsome as Lucas, and his hair was blond rather than black, but his smile was most charming. It lit up his pale blue eyes in a laughing manner. He bowed and kissed my hand. "Enchanted to meet you, my dear. If I may beg the honor of this dance?"

I curtsied, half intending to refuse, but he still held my hand. Rather than cause a scene, I agreed. I felt uneasy about the familiarity of his address, but Caroline's geniality and the fact that she actually introduced an available man to me put me off balance. I think I would have risked being rude if I had known the next dance was to be a waltz.

Though I felt I was well versed in dancing the waltz by this time, I felt uncomfortable with the way Sir Harlow danced it. It seemed he held me much too close for comfort, and his hand kept slipping up or down from where it should have been.

"Shall I felicitate you on acquiring an addition to your family?" he said.

I looked at him, a little puzzled at first. "Oh! You mean my stepfather, Sir Jeremy Swift. Yes, my mother married him not long ago."

"I believe their . . . attachment . . . was of long duration?"

I did not understand why he was asking me about my mother and Sir Jeremy. "I suppose so, Sir Harlow. Though I cannot comprehend why you should be interested in such private matters."

He smiled another charming smile. "I am sorry. It is just that I find you utterly captivating and cannot help but wonder about your own, ah, inclinations."

Before I knew what was happening, he swept me through some curtains out to a side balcony. He still held me close, and I found my chin firmly held in his hand. Startled, I looked up at him. The light outside was dim, but I could still see his expression, for the moon was full and very bright in addition to the brightness from within the house. A hungry look flashed in his eyes. Suddenly he pressed his mouth to mine. I stood frozen, panicky, not knowing what to do. "Lady Caroline's speculations were quite right," he murmured against my lips. "You are exquisite." His hand moved from my waist, and his fingers traced the edge of my décolletage.

At the touch of his hand and the sound of Caroline's name, I felt an enraged strength course through me. I pushed him forcefully away. His eyes widened, he yelped, and to my surprise, he disappeared. I heard a large splash down below. As my eyes grew more accustomed to the dimness, I saw that I was next to a low wall that formed the edge of the balcony. I remembered that Lord and Lady Amberley's house, which was just outside London, featured a wide moat around most of the building. Apparently Sir Harlow had fallen into it. I only wished Lady Caroline were here so I could push *her* in as well.

Shaking, I clenched and unclenched my hands, struggling for some control and composure. That wretched Caroline! How dare she! She must have told Sir Harlow something horrid about Mama and Sir Jeremy and no doubt hinted the same thing about me. Why else would he have taken advantage of me? I bit my lip in sudden anxiety. What *could* she have said about Mama and Sir Jeremy? And would it be something that others would think as well?

I looked over the balcony and watched to see if Sir Harlow would surface. He did. His blond hair reflected the light from the house and bobbed up and down as he swam to the edge of the moat. I breathed a sigh of relief. I would not want anyone hurt, no matter how angry I was. Then I stifled a laugh. Sir Harlow must have lost his coat in the water, for as he arose from the moat I could see his white shirt liberally striped with duck weeds. He was cursing dreadfully, if the half-inarticulate sounds from below were any indication. I saw Sir Harlow turning toward the balcony—no doubt to shake his fist at me—and I stepped back, not wanting him to see that I was still there.

I did not know how long exactly Sir Harlow and I had been on the balcony together, but I had to return. I smoothed back my hair as best I could, adjusted my bodice, and took a deep breath.

I put up my chin and pushed aside the curtains. To my dismay, the first eyes that met mine were Lucas's; the second, Lady Stoneham's. Lucas's expression was angry, and Lady Stoneham's was full of consternation. After being assaulted by Sir Harlow, I did not feel at all like confronting them. I admitted to cowardice: I looked about me for an escape.

I saw I could reach the entrance of the ball-room before either of them could reach me, so I slipped out those doors. I intended to go down the stairs, but then the front door to the mansion opened. I shrank down behind the balusters. It was a good thing I did: Sir Harlow entered. He must have had a remarkable store of oaths, for he was still cursing, and what was quite marvelous was that he did it in three languages.

As he shouted for a servant, opening one door after another, I could barely keep myself from laughing. He was still dripping water, and a dark, muddy stream coursed from him to the door. His shoes were surely ruined, for they squished noisily when he walked. He had taken off most of the duck weeds, but some still clung to him. As Sir Harlow stormed around the entrance hall, I could see that a large water lily was stuck to his back.

That was my undoing, for I could not suppress the snort of laughter that forced itself from behind my hands. His head came up and he shot a look so full of heated rage at me that I was sure I should have been burned to a crisp had his look been tangible. He started to climb up the stairs, his shoes squishing emphatically with each step.

It was a choice between the devil and the deep blue sea, so I chose to plunge once more into the ballroom. There, Lady Stoneham pounced upon me and opened her mouth to speak. "Georgia, how could you have gone—"

My gaze lit upon Sir Daniel, whom I had met earlier at Samantha's party, just two arms' lengths away. I smiled brilliantly upon him, willing him mentally to ask me to dance.

"Oh, I am *very* sorry, ma'am, but here is Sir Daniel come for our dance," I said hastily.

I thanked Providence that he *did* ask me. Our dance allowed me to gather some measure of composure, to where I no longer felt overwhelmed. I smiled gratefully at him at the end of the set, but then found that Providence apparently did not set much store in any of my mental utterances. For at the end of the music, I came face to face with Lucas.

"Our dance?" He did not look angry now, but he was still quite stern.

I quickly unfurled my fan, waving it in front of my face. "Oh, yes, I remember! But I fear I am overheated from the last one—perhaps we can sit this one out?" I looked at him hopefully over the top of my fan.

One corner of his mouth quirked up for a moment. "Well, as you wish. Perhaps some punch?" The stern look was gone. I sighed with relief. The thought that Lucas might be angry with me distressed me. After all, *I* had not done anything wrong—had I?

He led me to the punch bowl and put a glass in my hand. Then he turned to me. "Now, my girl, what were you doing—"

Suddenly a shock went through my elbow and cherry punch spilled over me. I stood still in horror as I watched the red seep like blood down the front of my dress, making the silk fabric cling indecently to my bosom. I turned to see who had done this. I could recognize the color of Lady Caroline's hair anywhere. Her back was turned to me, but the swirl of her skirts told me she hadn't been that way long. I yearned to tear out her carefully curled coiffure but knew I could not embarrass myself or Lucas with such a scene.

I turned again, this time facing Lucas. His eyes widened when he saw the stain and hurriedly brought me a cloth to dab at it. "It is of no use, Lucas," I said. "I am sorry, but I do not think I can remain here in this state."

He looked disappointed but said: "I suppose it can't be helped. Perhaps I can take you back to Lady Stoneham . . . ?"

Lady Stoneham. I must have grown pale, for he led me to a seat and bade me sit down. Not only had the dress she had chosen for me been slashed, but now the effort she had gone through to remedy that was also ruined. Then, too, she must have seen me leave the dance floor with Sir Harlow, and I suspected this was something she had not liked. I wished I did not have to face her, but that was the coward's way out, and I could not take that way again.

I looked up at Lucas. "Yes, I think I had better see her. It seems as if there is no help for it; I shall have to go home." I smiled as well as I could and stood up. I felt Lucas put my shawl around my shoulders and over the stain. It did not cover it. I smiled my thanks at him nevertheless.

Lucas patted my hand. "Well, it's not as if the ball has just begun. It lacks but an hour and a half to the end of it. Won't be such a loss if you leave now."

He led me back to Lady Stoneham, and though I could not make myself look at her, I clearly heard her gasp. "I cannot believe this. Don't speak to me, miss! My efforts were as nothing."

I lifted my eyes. "It was an accident!"

She rolled her eyes heavenward. "As was your earlier mishap! And then to disappear with— No, no! I do not want to hear more! There is nothing for it but that you must go home!"

"Lady Stoneham, I saw what happened." Lucas spoke up. "I assure you, ma'am, it was not Miss Canning's fault."

Lady Stoneham smiled at him. "Yes, yes. Quite gallant of you, Lord Ashcombe. But she cannot stay as she is. We must go home." She turned to look for Amelia, and annoyance passed quickly across Lucas's face.

He looked at me with an apologetic expression. "It will be all right, give you my word," he said.

I did not see what he could do about it, so I shrugged. "Oh, it is only a dress after all." There was my dance with Sir Harlow, too, but I said nothing about that. I looked down, pulling my shawl about me so that the stain would not show.

I continued to fiddle with it. I felt so despondent that I felt I could not look at Lucas. I heard Lady Stoneham's voice with a feeling of relief.

"Come, Georgia, Amelia. I must thank you, Lord Ashcombe, for standing by Georgia while I was away."

Lucas bowed formally, then glanced at me. "My pleasure, I assure you. I shall tell Samantha what happened; she will be sorry to miss you." He turned then and left. I fell even deeper in gloom. I knew I was in for a scold when we got back. Amelia looked smug. I think I really began to dislike her immensely from that point.

Of course I was scolded. I was not allowed to receive callers the next day, but that was just as well. I did not feel like talking with anyone. One bright occurrence was the arrival of my new dresses. I tried on one after another under Lady Stoneham's stern eye, and though she hovered about me as if I were going to spill some nonexistent drink upon them, my spirits lifted as I looked at all the different girls in the mirror. "No more accidents, my girl," she warned. "I know you are not clumsy, so how you came to ruin that dress is still a mystery to me. And disappearing with Sir Harlow—I thank Heaven that you did not reappear with him as well! I shall have to talk with your grandmama if this continues."

If I looked forward to balls with a certain amount of dread since the last one, at least my outings were free of it. Samantha called almost daily to drive or ride our horses in Hyde Park. This last sort of exercise was not my favorite, since I was not yet practiced at riding the sidesaddle. I had always thought it was a clumsy arrangement and looked at men astride with some envy. Occasionally, Lucas—now that he was back in town—would join us. Then it would almost be as it was before, the three of us, talking, joking, laughing. But still there was that little constraint, that little fence, between Lucas and me. I knew I loved him, but how did one act? What went beyond the line of what was pleasing? Did his kisses in the carriage mean he loved me or did I make too much of it? Or was it like the kiss of Sir Harlow, because there was something not quite right about me?

I didn't know whom to ask, was afraid to ask, in case what I had allowed to happen was of the grossest impropriety. I tried to put the whole issue from my mind. I didn't want to think of it. I just wanted to enjoy myself *now*.

I mentally shook myself and determinedly switched to a cheery frame of mind for the ride I was to have with Lucas one Monday morning. It was originally to have been with Samantha as well, but she had twisted her foot badly during the last ball, and it was still bruised. I had greeted this news with a raised eyebrow, but I made no demur. Lucas, after all, was Samantha's brother, I told myself, and I had known him longer than I had known her.

Annie roused me, and I quickly washed my face. I surreptitiously dabbed some essence of lavender behind my ears, even though the maid had turned her back. I laughed at myself. As if anyone cared whether I applied scent or not!

Annie chatted cheerily all the while and flung open my wardrobe as I put on my chemise. Her chattering stopped abruptly. I did not notice at first, for I was unknotting a ribbon, but then I turned. Annie stood as one struck, hands hanging limply at her sides, staring at my wardrobe. I felt definite foreboding at this odd behavior, but I moved to her side and my gaze followed her trembling, pointing finger.

I gasped. "Oh, Lord!" I murmured. The "phantom" slasher had struck again, but not with a scissors or knife: a liberal slash of ink now adorned everything in front of me. "Oh, Lord!" I backed away and sank hopelessly on my bed.

Annie turned to me, her face pale. "Lawks, miss! What are we going to do?"

I reached over and grasped her hand. "You needn't worry, Annie. I shall make sure you're not turned out for this. I know it's not your fault."

"But what about you, miss?"

"Well, I . . ." I stopped. I didn't know. This was the third time in a row an "accident" had happened, and this time it was to more than one dress. I glanced at the clock. It lacked but half an hour before my ride. "My riding habit, Annie. How badly dirtied is it?"

She gingerly pulled it from the wardrobe. It was a mess. Ink had been smeared from bodice to hem. "Could it be washed?" I ventured. It would be damp even if she could.

Annie hesitated. "I—I don't think so, miss, but I'll try!"

Twenty minutes passed while I paced back and forth in my room. What was I to say to Lady Stoneham? I had no real proof that Caroline or even Amelia was behind the destruction of my clothes. Further, I could not display any ingratitude for Lady Stoneham's presenting me to society by accusing Amelia to her mother—it would be a sure sign that Mama had brought me up badly. Any accusations would be useless. All I could say was that I did not know who had done it; but in the face of my obvious reluctance at the beginning to be parted from my mother, that explanation sounded quite lame. Anyone would be bound to think that a girl not long from school, obviously reluctant to be left with strangers, would be capable of mischief to get her way. And the viscountess had already named me headstrong and no doubt told Lady Stoneham so.

Annie knocked and entered. The look on her face told me all the washing in the world was not going to restore my riding habit to its former state. "Well—well, it seems that I am just going to have to have the headache and cry off." I smiled weakly. "When Lord Ashcombe arrives, please tell him for me, Annie, if you would be so kind."

I looked out my window and saw Lucas ride up and dismount. I couldn't suppress a spurt of frustrated anger; what else was I to do? Surely he would believe I was putting him off; a headache was such a clichéd excuse. And goodness only knew if anyone would believe me about my dresses. A few minutes passed and I saw him leave again—but not without company. A rider in a sky-blue habit rode up to him as he left, and a toss of her head revealed Caroline's face. My hands clenched. As if she had planned it—all so perfectly. As if—! I was sure from the top of my head to the tips of my toes that she *had* planned it. And there was nothing I could do about it.

11

I had no choice but to tell Lady Stoneham about my clothes. One could not have a headache forever, after all. And I made no excuses for it, other than to say that I did not know who had done it. It was, as I had thought, lame.

"Do not know who did it?" she exclaimed faintly. "They are your clothes, which—I had thought— you selected with such care. How could you not know who had—had *desecrated* them?" She raised vinaigrette to her nose and sneezed. "Why, when I was brought out, I could not take my eyes from my wardrobe! But you—!" A trembling hand was raised to cover her eyes. "Tearing your ball dress from bodice to hem was not enough, nor was spilling punch on the result of my creative genius. Possibly—*possibly,* I could see these might be accidents. But this—! This is naught but malice, my girl, malice! I respected the fact you did not want to be parted from your mother—very proper, indeed! But you need not have gone to such extremes as these!"

"But I didn't!" I cried.

"Then who did?" Lady Stoneham asked reasonably.

I fidgeted. "Lady Caroline," I said finally, goaded reluctantly into admitting my suspicion.

She looked at me sadly. "How could she have? They are your clothes, in your room, and you see them every day. How could she have done so?"

"I don't know," I said dully. "I do not know."

She tugged at her shawl discontentedly. "Well, I do not know what to do with you, girl. I cannot bring out a girl who constantly ruins her dresses."

"But I do not ruin my dresses—!" I cried.

Disbelief settled over her face. "If those dresses are not ruined, then I wonder why we are having this discussion."

"I mean—"

"Please!" moaned Lady Stoneham, holding up a hand. "No more! You fatigue me. I shall have to discuss this matter with your grandmama."

A sinking feeling grew in the pit of my stomach. I did not want the viscountess brought into this. She already thought me impertinent and headstrong, and nothing she had ever said led me to believe she had any affection for me. She would certainly voice those doubts Lady Stoneham had about me and believe them, too. And then what? I closed my eyes briefly. She would blame it all on Mama. Perhaps whisper it about that she did a horrible job raising me. Perhaps snub her in public. Or worse, never let me go back to her.

The viscountess's visit did nothing to dispel these fears. If I had thought her manner haughty when I first saw her, I now stood corrected. Her face was set in hard lines, her eyes chilly chips of ice. She had come calling in a black dress, outmoded but regal nevertheless. She said nothing for the first few minutes of our interview; her gaze went through me like a sword. I could not look at her for long, but a rebellious spark made me raise my chin again and I gazed at her as steadily as I could.

"Ungrateful!" she barked, and I jumped.

"No, ma'am." My voice squeaked just a little.

"'No, ma'am' what?"

"No, ma'am, I am not ungrateful."

"Not ungrateful! Not *ungrateful*!" The viscountess rose like a tidal wave from her chair.

I have never had a scolding in my life like the one I had from the viscountess. Mama had scolded me, but in her firm and gentle way, and I would always be sorry at the end. The viscountess's hand was like a vise on my arm as she pulled me toward her chair and made me stand in front of her. I had little time to reply to a question before she would snap out another one, and incredulity was writ large on her sharp features. I gave all the same answers I had given to Lady Stoneham, and before this matriarch they sounded weaker than ever.

Finally she let loose my arm and sat back. "You say you did not destroy your dresses, yet you do not know who did. It was not your maid, Annie, for she would have no cause, you say." She tapped her fingers on the arm of her chair. "Who do you *think* did it, then, if you do not know?"

I breathed a sigh of relief. Perhaps it was not as bad as I thought it would be. "I—I think it was Caroline Emmett-Johns. Perhaps Amelia," I said.

Lady Canning raised an eyebrow. "Proof?"

"I have little," I said. "It is just what I think. They are the only ones who would do those things to me. Caroline never did like me at school, and what she did, the others did also. Then, they had the opportunity when I was out with Samantha Ashcombe."

Lady Canning snorted. "They would not dare. You are a Canning. One does not perpetrate such tricks on a Canning."

"They would, ma'am, if they thought they could get away with it." I thought about how Lady Caroline had introduced Sir Harlow Smythe to me—no doubt Lady Stoneham had reported this to the viscountess as well. "And it was Lady Caroline who introduced me to Sir Harlow Smythe and told me I should dance with him."

"Humph! Did she now?" My grandmother tapped her fingers again, and a thoughtful look crossed her face—only briefly, however. "Well, you should have known better than to go off with him!" I opened my mouth to protest, but she continued relentlessly: "Besides, there is still no proof. And for all I know, you could be a very convincing liar."

I clenched my teeth. "I . . . am . . . not, my lady," I said slowly and deliberately.

"Your word means nothing to me, girl."

I lifted my chin. "I *am* a Canning, after all, ma'am. I don't lie."

Her fingers stopped their tapping, then continued again. "You are also your mother's daughter. I know nothing of her upbringing, and I can only suspect the worst."

"You never tried to know *anything* of her upbringing!" I spat out angrily. "How dare you judge her!"

"'How dare I—'" hissed her ladyship. "How dare you talk to me like that! I have confirmation of your upbringing from your own lips!" Her voice became calm, but her hand closed, white-knuckled, over her cane. "You are confined for three days in your room, no visitors, no parties."

"Confined!" I cried. "That is not fair! I have done nothing!"

"Five days, with bread and water only," returned the viscountess.

I shut my mouth, gnawing my lip in frustration. Clearly, the more I said, the worse it would be. I stood there, staring at her defiantly.

Having gained my silence, she smiled genially at me. "You may go."

The first day was not all that bad. I think Annie must have told my story to the cook, for I received large slabs of bread, and she managed to hide small scraps of roast beef in between them. The boredom, however, was excruciating. I had my

one book, *Pride and Prejudice,* which I finished
and started over again. I was not allowed out to
fetch another from the library, and Annie could
not get any, either, for she could not read well
enough to get the ones I wanted.

The second day became intolerable. I was hungry, for the bread, scraps, and water were less than
I was used to. But then, Caroline and Amelia were
so "kind" as to visit outside my door. Visit. It was
nothing but triumphant giggles and sly remarks, as
they were on their way to their routs and parties.
That was not so bad, but then Caroline said: "Ah, it
is too bad you cannot go to Lady Coventry's ball.
But you need not worry that you cannot go to it; I
shall make sure she knows why you cannot." She
laughed, and Amelia giggled. I said nothing. I hoped
they thought I was asleep. But sleep was far from
my mind, and I knew Caroline would be sure to
keep her promise and let all and sundry know I was
kept in my room for punishment.

I might as well be confined for the rest of my
life, I thought, furious. I cringed to think of the
speculative and pitying looks from people I was
sure to meet after my confinement. I felt my face
growing hot at the thought. I could not bear it. I
thought of the days to come; beyond the gossip
Caroline would spread, there would be more
mishaps engineered by Her Mischiefness, I was
sure of it. I would be confined again, perhaps sent
back to Mama in disgrace. I wished dreadfully I
was not in London. I wished I was back some-
where where I could be amongst my books and
papers, my paint pots and brushes, where I didn't

have to think of dresses that would inevitably be ruined. If I confined myself to my room, it would be because of my love of books and not by the will of a tyrant grandmother.

Books and paints, Plato and history. I wished I were in school again. *Then* I would not have to think of ruined dresses and balls and Caroline Emmett-Johns. . . . I sat up abruptly in my bed. Why not? I had done what Miss Angstead had wanted; Mama was now married to Sir Jeremy Swift. If I could not be a student again, perhaps Miss Angstead would let me be a schoolmistress! Surely she would take me in! Why, she *owed* it to me, after all! Did I not manage to tell Sir Jeremy the way he was to marry Mama? It was a thing the headmistress or any of her relatives were unable to do. Surely, at the very least, Miss Angstead should be able to find me a respectable position as a governess.

I sat still for a moment, thinking out a plan. I did not see how I could escape without being seen. And then there was the problem of proper chaperonage when I traveled. Even I—with my admittedly limited understanding of all that could go wrong in society's eyes—knew that. I could not take Annie, for she was also Amelia's maid, and I did not want her to be turned out because she agreed to help me.

Samantha! Of course *she* could not go with me, but perhaps she could let me borrow a servant. I did not want to impose on her good nature, but I felt sure that as my friend, Samantha would understand. Our minds worked very similarly, I thought, and she would comprehend my predicament in an instant. I sat down at a table and wrote out a brief letter, explaining my situation. I waited for Annie to bring up my supper.

"Annie, wait!" I said, holding on to her arm. She looked at me fearfully.

"Miss Georgia, I can't! I'm expected belowstairs." She stared nervously at her toes.

"Only a minute. I need to send a note to my friend Miss Ashcombe—I, I borrowed something, so I need to let her know why I cannot return it. Could you take it to her for me—with—without anyone knowing about it? I know I can trust you, Annie, please do it for me!"

Annie bit her lip, then looked up at me. "I shouldn't, miss, but, well, you did stand up for me and took the blame for those dresses." She put her hand on mine and patted it. "I'll do it."

I squeezed her hand. "Thank you, Annie." She almost protested when I slipped a coin in her hand, but I closed her fingers around it and pushed her out the door.

The next day was worse than tedious. It was nerve-racking. I paced my room anxiously, waiting for a word from Samantha. Finally, Annie came up with my monotonous repast. She looked about the room furtively, then handed me a letter.

"Here, Miss Georgia. Their footman, Robin, gave it to me." She flushed a bright pink when she mentioned the footman's name. I refrained from smiling but gave her another shilling.

"Thank you, Annie. I shall not forget this." But then I couldn't resist teasing a little. "You might think about buying a ribbon with it, Annie," I said. "A pink one. You would look becoming in pink." Annie blushed more furiously than ever but grinned at me as she curtsied and left.

I broke the letter's seal with eager hands.

"My Dear Georgia," I read. "How perfectly Odious of your Grandmother to keep you Confined, a Prisoner in your Own Room—how Terribly Unjust of her! Anyone with a Modicum of Intelligence could see that *you* could not have Ruined your Dresses. Of course, I shall help you! Be ready at Ten O'clock Tonight, and I will send someone to aid your escape from your Dastardly Imprisonment. As you suggested, I shall Instruct that you be awaited under your Window. Your Most Concerned Friend, Samantha."

I could hardly eat my luncheon in my relief and excitement; not that there was much to eat— bread and water, with just a bit of beef hidden, as before. I busied myself, putting together what I would need for my escape.

I searched through my wardrobe for some clothes not too badly stained by the ink. I pulled two bandboxes from under my bed and folded all the necessary things in them: toothbrush, cup, hairbrush . . . Jewelry! I must take that, too, just in case my pin money was not enough for the mail coach. I packed things quickly, not neatly; I did not care. Once Samantha's and my scheme was laid out, I could not be held back.

I made sure my bandboxes were well hidden under my bed when supper—bread and water again—arrived. I ate some of the bread, then frugally put the rest in a handkerchief in my reticule. My stomach growled and twinged in protest. I could not be sure, however, that my small fund of pin money and jewelry would last until I reached Bath. I continued packing. I debated between a hooded cloak and a pelisse with a bonnet. I decided on a cloak with a hood large enough to cover a small bonnet. One could never be sure what one would need when on a journey.

I looked at the clock on the mantelpiece. It wanted but five minutes to ten o'clock. I pulled the bedclothes from my bed, tying the corners tightly together. I had read of this method of escape in one of Mama's novels. I swallowed as I opened my window and looked down. While I could tolerate heights, I did not care for them. But my makeshift rope was long enough.

I made sure once again the knots in the bed-sheets were tied together firmly, then lowered the rope out my window. A soft rustle told me the rope had reached the tall bushes below. I smiled to myself in grim satisfaction. Only about a two-foot drop from there; I need not fear any injury.

I hesitated only a second about the disposition of my bandboxes before I tied them about my waist. I giggled as I caught sight of myself in the mirror. My cloak stretched out around them, and I looked for all the world as though I were one of those old-fashioned ladies who wore panniers on either side of their hips under their dresses. I firmly secured the rope to the bedpost and tied on my bonnet.

Carefully, carefully, I lowered myself down the

rope. It was dark, but the moon was full, so I could see that the street was deserted; no one would detect what I was about.

Suddenly I heard footsteps around the corner to my left. Perhaps it was the servant Samantha was to send me—or perhaps it was a stranger. Alarmed, I hesitated. I could not go back up, I could only go down as quickly as I could. I looked hurriedly down to see if the owner of the footsteps had come around the corner yet. That was a mistake. Hunger and vertigo hit me with almost a physical slap and the world split in two and I fell. . . .

"Ooof! What the devil?"

This was not the cobblestone beneath my window; cobblestone did not feel like Bath superfine and did not say "Ooof!" much less swear. I lay where I was for a few seconds, then, satisfied I was not more than bruised, stood up. Or tried to. A large hand grasped my arm and pulled me down again. "Good God! Who do you think you are, running down a man like that in the middle of the night, eh? Like a cannon shot! Bowled me over! Now I'll have to go back home and change again!"

"Lucas!" I exclaimed.

"Georgia?" Two hands grasped my arms and helped me to my feet. "Good God, what are you doing out here?"

"Oh, Lucas!" I said, tears coming involuntarily to my eyes. "I'm so sorry!"

"Now, now, my dear girl, don't cry! You never cry! Remember you said so once!" He fumbled for a handkerchief but did not seem to find one. He looked at me helplessly, then wiped my tears with his hand. "Now what is this about?"

"I am sorry I am crying. I have been perfectly miserable, and I suppose I am a little shaken from falling from the window. . . ."

"From the window!" His eyes traveled up the side of the house to the open casement. "Good God, girl! You might have killed yourself!" A look of horror dawned on his face. "Was this why Samantha—? Was it something I did? The constraint between us—I didn't think—I knew I went over the line in that carriage, I—I thought you cared for me a little—" He raised a hand as if to touch my face but stopped just short of it. "The cleverest girl I've ever met—but should have remembered how much an innocent you still are. I am sorry—"

I stared at him, openmouthed and confused. "Lucas, no, really, I did not mind, I mean, it is not because of the, well, ah, our kiss!"

He frowned. "Then why the devil did you jump out of your window? Was it—was it because of Sir Harlow?" Lucas's eyes grew stormy. "By God, if he has done anything to harm you, he'll have to answer to *me*!"

I blushed. "Oh, no! He did take me out to the balcony and kiss me, but *that* is not why I was at the window! I made a rope and *climbed* out of the window, only I became dizzy and lost hold toward the end. I am running away to Miss Angstead's Seminary."

I think I have never faced true anger before this. My mother's scolds and the viscountess's cross-examination were nothing compared to Lucas's fury. I found myself seized by my shoulders and soundly shaken.

"God help me, if I didn't know what an innocent you are, I would swear you were trying to ruin yourself, or worse, on purpose!" Lucas ground out, his jaw clenched. "How could you let him kiss you? Do you not know— Good God! Think, Georgia! Think! Sir Harlow is a *rake*. And there are many more like him, altogether eager to take advantage of someone like you. What's more, how are you going to get to Miss Angstead's? Where are you going to get the money to procure tickets? And who is going to protect you when you go? You have lived in London before this—do you still not know how dangerous it can be?"

I looked away from him so I could contain myself, for though I was a little frightened, I was angry, too. How dare he shake me! "You needn't speak to me as if I were a stupid schoolgirl! I am going by mail coach, I shall pay with the jewels I have, and Samantha is sending a servant to accompany me. And I *have* learned about men like Sir Harlow. I don't need anyone to protect me!" I said defiantly.

Lucas put his hand to his head, clutching a stray lock of hair in frustration. "No?" he retorted, and his hand sliced the air, gesturing at the street. "Look about you. I don't see a servant. It is dark, only the lamp above us for light. The walk's long to the nearest posting house. What if it wasn't me you met here, eh? Don't you know what could happen to you? Don't you know how beautiful you are?"

"Beautiful?" I looked up at him. Anger and fear crossed his features still. "Oh, no, I am not beautiful at all, Lucas. You have said it before, I know, but I cannot conceive how you can think so! You must know that Mama is the one who—"

"The devil fly away with your mother! I wish I had never— Oh, damn it all!" he cried despairingly, and pulled me hard into his arms.

I could not explain anything to him at all. It is impossible to speak when a man's lips are crushed to yours, kissing you breathless. After a while, I did not want to. I grew dizzy again, but I was not at all sure if it was because of hunger or because he held me so tightly. My knees shivered, and somehow it seemed a good notion to hold on to him. My arms crept slowly around his neck, pulling him closer to me. He felt warm in this cool night, and his greatcoat made a shelter around us.

"Damned bonnet!" I heard him growl, and I felt it tumble from my head. I did not care. Warm hands under my cloak caressed my back and shoulders, and the electric sensation banished all thought of bonnets. It followed the course of his hands down to my waist and—

Something bumped insistently on both sides of my hips. "What the devil—!" exclaimed Lucas. I was suddenly released.

I giggled. "My bandboxes. I tied them to my waist so I could use both hands for climbing."

"Climbing?" Lucas gazed at me, confused.

"I told you, I'm running away."

"Running away!" He gazed at the rope and back at me again. He looked bemused. "Thank God I

was the one you ran into!" he said fervently, kissing me again.

"Oh, yes!" I said, catching my breath as his
lips crept across my cheek and down past my
neck. My cloak had loosened a little. I heard the
bandboxes dropping to the ground. I also thought
I heard some footsteps in the distance. "I—I
don't think we should be standing here like this,
Lucas. Samantha's servant should be here any
moment."

"Eh?" He looked around, bewildered. "Ah, yes."
He straightened his greatcoat. The footsteps
came closer: it was the watch, and we waited in
what I hoped was an innocuous manner until he
passed us.

"I suppose I should escort you home," said
Lucas.

I looked pleadingly at him. "I cannot. I will not
stay with Lady Stoneham anymore. I am running
away to Miss Angstead's."

"I thought you were finished there."

I sighed. "I am, but I thought I might get a position as a schoolmistress."

"Why?" he said bluntly.

I hesitated. "I know you—you are fond of Caroline Emmett-Johns, Lucas—"

"Fond! Not likely!"

"Do—do you love her, then?"

"Good God, no!"

A warm feeling came over me, but I said, "But
she's so pretty! How can you not?"

"Passable, but rather pushing and insipid, really."

"And I," I said eagerly, "I am not?"

He grinned and drew me to him again. "No, especially not when you kiss like that!" he said when we parted.

"Well, she might kiss better than I, though, Lucas," I said mischievously.

Lucas shook his head, and his grin grew wider. "No, I doubt it. Her lips do not look at all as kissable as yours."

My eyes fell and I blushed, but I brought the conversation back firmly. "Well, then, about Lady Caroline. I do not like to be a talebearer, but . . ." I told him briefly about the last couple of weeks. "I do not have any proof she or Amelia did it, but I cannot help but think it! And then it was Caroline who introduced Sir Harlow to me, and said that I should dance with him."

"And you listened to her, after all you suspected of her?"

"Well, she took me by surprise, and Sir Harlow took my hand for the dance before I could think! Besides, no one told me I should avoid him!" In view of my weak explanation, I had to admit Lucas's skeptical expression was somewhat justified. "But I rid myself of him well enough, I assure you!"

"Oh?" Lucas still looked skeptical.

"If you *must* know, I pushed him over the balcony into the moat!" I retorted, much goaded.

"Good God!" uttered Lucas, sounding shocked.

"Well, it was only what he deserved, after all!" I said defensively. "And I do not know why Sir Harlow should have looked so surprised. He should have expected it after trying to kiss me!"

There was a short silence.

"Oh . . . my . . . God!" Lucas threw back his head and let out a shout of laughter.

"And after he swam out," I said, trying hard not to giggle, "he had duck weeds all over him!"

Lucas went into another spasm of mirth.

"Then when he came back to L-Lord Amberley's house, h-his sh-shoes s-squished." I started to hiccup with the effort not to laugh. "A-and he had a water lily s-stuck to his back!"

Lucas let out a very ungentlemanly howl of laughter, and I could not help myself—I whooped until my stomach hurt and I had to hold on to him for support. Finally we settled down, though it only took a glance to start us off again. We looked about us. My bandboxes had rolled a few feet away, though my bonnet was still at my feet.

"Hmmm." Lucas gathered up my bandboxes and gave me my bonnet. I tied it back on, looking at him expectantly. "Not a good time for a lady to be out alone. I'll take you to Mater's. Samantha will be glad to see you; she's been a bit moped from a cold as well as from her foot." He drew my hand through the crook of his arm.

"Y-your mother's!" I stammered. "But I cannot!"

"Why not?" he asked reasonably.

"Well, the servant Samantha is sending for me, what of that?" I stalled.

"There isn't any servant. Samantha sent me."

"What!" I stared openmouthed at him. "But I asked to borrow a servant!"

Lucas shook his head. "Sam said you needed help. Said you were in 'dire straits' or some such fustian. Thought she might be roasting me, but I couldn't be sure she wasn't sincere. So, I had to come." A thought seemed to occur to him, for a frown creased his forehead.

"Well . . ." I hesitated, for I felt there was something that was not quite right, but I could not put my finger on it. "Well, it would not be seemly if I were to run from Lady Stoneham's to come to your mother, who is not related to me at all!"

"It isn't seemly to run to Miss Angstead's, either! Anyway, there's no need to make it known that you had run away. It's perfectly respectable for you to stay at a friend's house. And if we were betrothed, why, that would be unexceptional."

"Betrothed!" I said faintly, and clutched his arm. The street seemed to take a quick spin. "You—you mean if we were to let it about that we were betrothed—"

"I should think we would want it to be known sooner or later. Things like that are not kept secret for long, you know."

I stopped in my tracks. "Lucas! Are you saying you want to *marry* me?"

He turned to me, smiling wistfully. "Thought you might like it better than teaching at Miss Angstead's. And if you still want to teach, I *am* starting a mill school on one of my estates."

I could not look at him. "You needn't offer for me just because you feel sorry for me, or because you felt obliged to kiss me. I can do very well at Miss Angstead's; I'm quite self-reliant, you know—"

His finger lifted my chin, and I looked into his eyes. He bent and kissed me long and hard. "Stupid," he said caressingly. "Do you think I would kiss you like that if I didn't love you?"

"Oh, Lucas! I have loved you for so *very* long!" I cried, and flung my arms around his neck. I heard the bandboxes drop as he used his hands to a much better purpose.

Despite my delight in this renewed bout of kissing, the thought that had grown in the back of my mind finally flowered. "Lucas! I have just realized! I believe Samantha has meant to have us betrothed all along!" I exclaimed indignantly when his lips left mine. "She arranged our carriage ride, and sent you here instead of a servant, after all."

"That occurred to me as well. In fact, I am sure of it. My sister is a scheming minx," murmured Lucas against my ear. "Shall we strangle her?"

"Oh, no! I am sure she meant it for the best," I said in a rather breathless voice. "Besides, one can only admire such Planning and Strategy!"

The sound of faint voices startled us, and we parted. "We should go," said Lucas.

We started away from Lady Stoneham's house, but my betrothed stopped suddenly. Lucas looked at the house and shook his head. "One moment!" He walked back to it and seemed to search the ground for something. He fumbled with the end of the bedsheet rope, then with a great heave threw the end of it back into my window. I heard a slight crash, which may have been a chair just sitting opposite to the window. "There!" he said, satisfied. "Bad *ton* having something like that hanging from one's window."

AVAILABLE NOW

ONE NIGHT by Debbie Macomber

A wild, romantic adventure from bestselling and much-loved author Debbie Macomber. When their boss sends them to a convention in Dallas together, Carrie Jamison, a vibrant and witty radio deejay for KUTE in Kansas City, Kansas, and Kyle Harris, an arrogant, strait-laced KUTE reporter, are in for the ride of their lives, until one night. . . . "Debbie Macomber writes delightful, heartwarming romances that touch the emotions and leave the reader feeling good."—Jayne Ann Krentz

MAIL-ORDER OUTLAW by Millie Criswell

From the award-winning author of *Phantom Lover* and *Diamond in the Rough*, a historical romance filled with passion, fun, and adventure about a beautiful New York socialite who found herself married to a mail-order outlaw. "Excellent! Once you pick it up, you won't put it down."—Dorothy Garlock, bestselling author of *Sins of Summer*

THE SKY LORD by Emma Harrington

When Dallas MacDonald discovered that his ward and betrothed had run off and married his enemy, Ian MacDougall, he was determined to fetch his unfaithful charge even if it meant war. But on entering Inverlocky Castle, Dallas found more pleasure in abducting MacDougall's enchanting sister, Isobel, than in securing his own former betrothed.

WILLOW CREEK by Carolyn Lampman

The final book in the Cheyenne Trilogy. Given her father's ill health during the hot, dry summer of 1886, Nicki Chandler had no choice but to take responsibility for their Wyoming homestead. But when her father hired handsome drifter Levi Cantrell to relieve some of her burdens, the last thing Nicki and Levi ever wanted was to fall in love.

PEGGY SUE GOT MURDERED by Tess Gerritsen

Medical examiner M. J. Novak, M.D., has a problem: Too many bodies are rolling into the local morgue. She teams up with the handsome, aristocratic president of a pharmaceutical company, who has his own agenda. Their search for the truth takes them from glittering ballrooms to perilous back alleys and into a romance that neither ever dreamed would happen.

PIRATE'S PRIZE by Venita Helton

A humorous and heartwarming romance set against the backdrop of the War of 1812. Beautiful Loire Chartier and dashing Dominique Youx were meant for each other. But when Loire learned that Dominique was the half brother of the infamous pirate, Jean Lafitte, and that he once plundered her father's cargo ship, all hell broke loose.

COMING NEXT MONTH

CIRCLE IN THE WATER by Susan Wiggs

When a beautiful gypsy thief crossed the path of King Henry VIII, the king saw a way to exact revenge against his enemy, Stephen de Lacey, by forcing the insolvent nobleman to marry the girl. Stephen wanted nothing to do with his gypsy bride, even when he realized Juliana was a princess from a far-off land. But when Juliana's past returned to threaten her, he realized he would risk everything to protect his wife. "Susan Wiggs creates fresh, unique and exciting tales that will win her a legion of fans."—Jayne Ann Krentz

JUST ONE OF THOSE THINGS by Leigh Riker

Sara Reid, having left her race car driver husband and their glamorous but stormy marriage, returns to Rhode Island in the hope of protecting her five-year-old daughter from further emotional harm. Instead of peace, Sara finds another storm when her husband's cousin Colin McAllister arrives—bringing with him the shameful memory of their one night together six years ago and a life-shattering secret.

DESTINED TO LOVE by Suzanne Elizabeth

In the tradition of her first time travel romance, *When Destiny Calls*, comes another humorous adventure. Josie Reed was a smart, gutsy, twentieth-century doctor, and tired of the futile quest for a husband before she reached thirty. Then she went on the strangest blind date of all—back to the Wild West of 1881 with a fearless, half-Apache, bounty hunter.

A TOUCH OF CAMELOT by Donna Grove

The winner of the 1993 Golden Heart Award for best historical romance. Guinevere Pierce had always dreamed that one day her own Sir Lancelot would rescue her from a life of medicine shows and phony tent revivals. But she never thought he would come in the guise of Cole Shepherd, the Pinkerton detective in charge of watching over Gwin and her younger brother Arthur, the only surviving witnesses to a murder.

SUNFLOWER SKY by Samantha Harte

A poignant historical romance between an innocent small town girl and a wounded man bent on vengeance. Sunny Summerlin had no idea what she was getting into when she rented a room to an ill stranger named Bar Landry. But as she nursed him back to health, she discovered that he was a bounty hunter with an unquenchable thirst for justice, and also the man with whom she was falling in love.

TOO MANY COOKS by Joanne Pence

Somebody is spoiling the broth in this second delightful adventure featuring the spicy romantic duo from *Something's Cooking*. Homicide detective Paavo Smith must find who is killing the owners of popular San Francisco restaurants and, at the same time, come to terms with his feelings for Angelina Amalfi, the gorgeous but infuriating woman who loves to dabble in sleuthing.

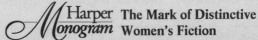 **Harper Monogram** The Mark of Distinctive Women's Fiction